Leader of the in crowd . . .

"OK, Brian," Mr. Levin said, facing the tough-looking boy who had just moved to Sweet Valley from Los Angeles. "I want you to choose eleven people and have them all stand against the wall on the right."

"Uh . . . OK, Aaron Dallas, Ken Matthews, the Wakefield girls . . . " Brian began. He smiled at the twins mischievously.

This is totally cool, *Jessica thought as she and Elizabeth joined the others against the wall.* It's like we're being chosen for a club or something.

As Brian continued listing names, Jessica became more and more excited—he was choosing all the coolest kids.

"As the leader of your team, you're going to make up the rules that everyone has to follow," Mr. Levin told Brian once he had selected eleven people. "And if you decide someone can't be in your group anymore, then they're out."

"This sounds pretty awesome," Brian said, a huge smile spreading across his face.

SWEET VALLEY TWINS

It Can't Happen Here

Written by
Jamie Suzanne

Created by
FRANCINE PASCAL

BANTAM BOOKS
NEW YORK • TORONTO • LONDON • SYDNEY • AUCKLAND

RL 4, 008-012

IT CAN'T HAPPEN HERE
A Bantam Book / April 1995

Sweet Valley High® and Sweet Valley Twins™ are registered trademarks of Francine Pascal

Conceived by Francine Pascal

Produced by Daniel Weiss Associates, Inc.
33 West 17th Street
New York, NY 10011

Cover art by James Mathewuse

ISBN: 0-553-48113-4

Published simultaneously in the United States and Canada

Bantam Books are published by Bantam Books, a division of Bantam Doubleday Dell Publishing Group, Inc. Its trademark, consisting of the words "Bantam Books" and the portrayal of a rooster, is Registered in the U.S. Patent and Trademark Office and in other countries. Marca Registrada. Bantam Books, 1540 Broadway, New York, New York 10036.

PRINTED IN THE UNITED STATES OF AMERICA

OPM 0 9 8 7 6 5 4 3 2 1

To Isabella Leitner,
author of the young-adult book
Fragments of Isabella,
A Memoir of Auschwitz.

One

"Hey, Aaron, it's me," Ken Matthews said to Aaron Dallas over the phone. "You still up for tonight?"

Aaron smiled and sat down on the top stair in the upstairs hallway of his house. "Totally. I wouldn't miss it," he answered.

It was Friday evening, and Aaron was looking forward to a night out at the Valley Mall with a bunch of his friends from Sweet Valley Middle School. Practically everyone was going to be there, including a new, really cool guy from L.A. named Brian Boyd. They'd planned to meet for pizza, then go to a movie.

"Cool. I'm heading out now," Ken said. "I'll see you in a few minutes."

Aaron hung up the phone and bounded down the stairs. "Bye!" he called to his parents and grandfather, who were in the dining room.

"Aaron!" his grandfather called in his slight German accent.

Reluctantly, Aaron shut the door and walked slowly into the dining room.

"Where are you going?" his grandfather, Mr. Kramer, asked, raising his eyebrows inquisitively.

Aaron sighed. He didn't really have time to shoot the breeze with his grandfather, who was visiting Sweet Valley from New Jersey while he recovered from heart surgery. When Aaron was younger, he would've been completely psyched to have his grandfather around for two whole weeks. His grandfather was his hero. He was always doing really funny magic tricks, and he used to take Aaron on fishing trips.

But things were different now. It wasn't that he loved his grandfather any less. Now that he was older, Aaron liked to hang with his friends and didn't have as much time to sit around and watch magic tricks.

"I'm going to meet my friends for a pizza and a movie," Aaron said quickly, hoping his grandfather would get the message.

Mr. Kramer smiled at Aaron. "You forgot we were having Sabbath dinner, my boy."

Aaron felt his heart drop. He *had* completely forgotten, even though his Grandpa had been talking about the dinner all week. But he couldn't miss out on the night with his friends—especially because this was a great opportunity to get to know Brian.

"Listen," Aaron said, thinking fast, "I'll have dinner with you guys tomorrow, OK? My friends are waiting for me."

"Sorry, honey, but you're eating dinner with us tonight," Mrs. Dallas said. "You can join your friends later. I'm sure they'll understand if you have important dinner plans."

"But we never have a Sabbath dinner," Aaron protested.

"We're having one tonight," Mr. Dallas said. "Grandpa's been cooking all afternoon."

"And everything looks absolutely delicious, Dad," Mrs. Dallas said to her father.

Aaron sighed. From the looks on his parents' faces, he could tell it would be pointless to argue any more. *Fine,* he thought. *I'll just eat really fast, then get out of here. How long can it take to eat dinner?*

"Hey, can I borrow something to wear tonight?" Jessica Wakefield asked her identical twin sister, Elizabeth, on Friday night after dinner.

Elizabeth was sitting on her bed reading. She looked up from her book in a daze. "Hmmmm . . . sure . . . whatever," she mumbled.

"Excuse me, Nerd of America, but didn't you get the message that it's Friday night?" Jessica asked, shaking her head. "There's a law that says you're not supposed to study on Friday nights."

Elizabeth rolled her eyes and closed her book. "I guess I'm getting really into this week's social studies reading. It's about the beginning of World War Two."

"Sounds fascinating," Jessica said dryly as she opened Elizabeth's closet.

"It is," Elizabeth insisted. "I'm sure even *you'll* find it interesting."

"No, I think you're interested enough for both of us," Jessica said as she pulled a pink sweater out of Elizabeth's closet. "Maybe I'll just let you read it for me."

Elizabeth had to laugh. *Typical Jessica,* she thought. On the outside, Elizabeth and Jessica looked exactly alike. They both had long blond hair and blue-green eyes. They even had the same dimple in their left cheeks. But the similarities ended there.

Elizabeth was much more serious about her schoolwork than Jessica was. In fact, she'd recently skipped to the seventh grade since she'd been doing such a good job in all her sixth-grade classes. After a couple of weeks, however, she realized that even though she could handle the seventh grade academically, she wasn't ready for all the social pressures.

In her free time, Elizabeth loved to read and write. She was the editor-in-chief of the *Sixers*, the sixth-grade newspaper she helped start, and she wanted to be a writer when she grew up. She also loved having long talks with her close friends Amy Sutton and Maria Slater, who both worked with her on the *Sixers*.

Jessica was always teasing Elizabeth about her friends—she thought they were incredibly boring. Elizabeth, on the other hand, was always teasing

Jessica about how silly *her* friends were. Jessica was a member of the Unicorn Club, a group made up of the prettiest and most popular girls at Sweet Valley Middle School. It seemed to Elizabeth that all they ever talked about were clothes, parties, and boys. But even though they had totally different interests, Elizabeth and Jessica were as close as two sisters could be.

"This looks nice with my hair, don't you think?" Jessica asked, holding up her twin's sweater in front of her.

"Beautiful," Elizabeth agreed with a smile. "As nice as it does with *my* hair. In fact, I was planning on wearing it tonight." She jumped up and removed the sweater from her sister's clutches.

"You're wearing it to study in your bedroom?" Jessica teased.

"Ha ha ha," Elizabeth said as she slipped the sweater over her head. "For your information, I'm wearing it to Amy's house. Maria's coming over, too, and we're going to rent a movie."

Jessica put her hand over her mouth and faked a dramatic yawn. "Gee, that really sounds like a wild and crazy Friday night. I'm about to fall asleep just thinking about it."

"So what are you doing that's so much more exciting?" Elizabeth asked.

Jessica held up a white button-down shirt and looked in the mirror. "Well, the Unicorns are getting together with some of the guys for pizza and a movie," she said, throwing the shirt on the floor. "And I *was* going to invite you to join us. That new guy, Brian Boyd, is going to be there."

Elizabeth leaned over and picked up the shirt. "I don't see what the big deal is about that guy. I mean, when he walked into the lunchroom today, the whole school practically flipped out."

Jessica shook her head in disbelief as she rummaged through Elizabeth's closet. "It sometimes amazes me that we're sisters, Lizzie. You obviously have no appreciation for coolness."

"I guess I don't," Elizabeth agreed, folding her arms. "And since you obviously know so much about it, maybe you could tell me what's so cool about Brian Boyd."

"Well, the way he dresses, for one thing," Jessica explained. "Like that leather jacket and the way he always wears his baseball cap turned backwards. Also, he uses really hip expressions—you know, he's just cool."

Elizabeth frowned. "So you're telling me that people are going so crazy over him because of the way he wears his baseball cap and because of a few expressions he uses?"

Jessica gave her sister an impatient look. "Don't ask me to explain the essence of coolness to you, Lizzie. You'll just have to come out with us tonight so you can see for yourself."

Elizabeth laughed, even though she felt a little weird about this whole "cool" business. *Cool* was a word that always bugged her. In her opinion, being cool meant being a nice, interesting person, but she knew that it had a whole different meaning to Jessica and her friends.

Elizabeth had tried being what most people would consider "cool" when she was in the seventh grade, but she learned that she preferred just being herself—even if that meant *not* being cool.

"Thanks for the invitation, Jess, but I think I'll pass," Elizabeth said, pulling her hair back into a ponytail. "I think I'll just hang out with my boring, uncool friends."

"Suit yourself," Jessica said as she slipped on Elizabeth's sleeveless denim shirt. "But I guarantee you that I'm going to have a much better time than you are tonight."

"I'll just have to live with that," Elizabeth said, smiling.

"Aaron, please read the second prayer on page fifty-two," Mr. Kramer instructed.

Aaron looked at his watch and groaned to himself. *This is the longest dinner in history,* he thought. It was eight o'clock, fifteen minutes before the movie was supposed to start, and it didn't look as though he was going to get there anytime soon.

He looked down at the prayer book. "This is in Hebrew," he complained.

"The English translation is at the bottom of the page," Mr. Kramer pointed out.

Aaron read the prayer quickly, barely paying any attention to what he was saying. When he finished, he put down the book and looked up at his mother. "Can I go now?"

"You always were a restless boy," Mr. Kramer said affectionately. "First, we should talk about the meaning of what you have just read."

"Grandpa's right," Mr. Dallas said. "Sit still."

I feel like I'm in school, Aaron thought, as he slumped back down in his chair.

"Over the centuries, Jews have been persecuted because of what they are," Mr. Kramer started. "That prayer—"

"But that's all in the past," Aaron said, squirming in his seat. "What's the point in remembering all of that now?"

Grandpa's face turned serious and sad. "We *have* to remember the past," he said somberly. "That is the only way we can make sure that such things as the Holocaust never happen again."

"But nothing like that could ever happen here," Aaron said dismissively. His grandfather was the only person he knew who ever talked about the Holocaust, and Aaron never paid that much attention to what he said. It was something that seemed so long ago and so far off.

"It could happen anywhere at any time," Mr. Kramer said as he folded his hands on top of his prayer book. "It could even happen here."

Two

"What time does your movie start?" Mr. Kramer asked Aaron when dinner was finally over.

"It starts in ten minutes," Aaron mumbled. He knew that even if he rode his bike as fast as possible, he still wouldn't make it to the theater in time.

"Well, let's hurry up and I'll take you there," Mr. Kramer offered.

Aaron's face lit up. "Thanks, Grandpa! If you drive, I'll make it there in time."

"What kind of movie is it?" Mr. Kramer asked.

"It's science-fiction horror," Aaron said excitedly. "It's called *Dead Thing, Part Four*."

"I love movies like that," Mr. Kramer said as they headed toward the front hallway.

"Really?" Aaron asked, stifling a laugh. His

grandfather didn't exactly seem like the kind of person who liked horror movies.

"Those movies are always full of surprises," Mr. Kramer said, grinning broadly. "And you know what? Since I'm driving you, why don't I stay and see this one with you? Afterwards, I could take you and your friends for ice cream."

Aaron stopped in his tracks. It was really sweet of his grandfather to want to meet his friends, but he knew it wouldn't go over too well—Brian would think he was a big dork for showing up with his grandpa.

Aaron was about to tell his grandfather that it would be better if he just dropped him off, when he saw the look on the old man's face. He was wearing his old tweed cap, and he was happily jingling the car keys in his hand. *He looks really excited—I can't just tell him I don't want him around.*

Aaron put his hand over his mouth and yawned loudly. "You know what, Grandpa?" he said, "I suddenly feel exhausted. I guess I'm not up to going to the movie, after all."

Grandpa looked confused. "But your friends," he started, "they're waiting for you, no?"

Aaron shuffled back and forth. "That's OK. There's a whole group of them, so I'm sure nobody will really care if I don't show up."

"All right. Well, would you like to watch a movie on TV instead?" Mr. Kramer suggested. "Maybe we could rent something at the tape store."

"You mean the video store," Aaron corrected, feeling a stab of annoyance. He hadn't noticed it when he was younger, but now it bugged him the way Grandpa was always using the wrong expression for things. "No, I think I'll just go right to bed," he said quickly. "Good night."

"What a totally disgusting movie," Jessica said after she took the last loud slurp of her chocolate milk shake. "I almost lost it when that creature with three heads popped out of that refrigerator."

It was later that night, and Jessica was sitting with her fellow Unicorns in a booth at Casey's, a popular ice cream parlor in Sweet Valley. The guys were sitting in the next booth, and Jessica was talking extra loudly for the benefit of one particular guy—Brian Boyd.

"I kind of liked it," Lila Fowler said. "Especially the love story part."

Lila was Jessica's best friend after Elizabeth, and she and Jessica were super-competitive with each other. Lila was one of the wealthiest girls in Sweet Valley. It got on Jessica's nerves that Lila had so many great clothes. And it *really* irked her when Lila disagreed with her in public.

"What love story?" Jessica asked, sitting back in the booth and crossing her arms in front of her. "Did you sneak into another movie or something? There sure wasn't a love story in the movie I just saw."

"How can you say that?" Lila asked, flipping her long brown hair over her shoulder. "Those two creatures were having a total romance. They did that whole dance together and everything."

Jessica let out a loud laugh. "You must be joking," she said.

"Excuse me, but I couldn't help eavesdropping," Brian said, as he turned around in his booth and looked at Jessica and her friends. "Are you talking about the way those creatures were throwing the doughnuts around?"

Jessica felt her cheeks grow warm. Brian was totally handsome—he had thick, dark hair and broad shoulders. Plus he was really charming, and that made him seem older than the other guys in the sixth grade. Jessica wasn't exactly looking for a boyfriend. She was sort of going out with Aaron Dallas, and she was really crazy about him. Still, she couldn't help being attracted to Brian.

Lila flashed a bright smile in Brian's direction. "*Exactly*—the doughnut dance," she said, meeting his eyes. "Wasn't that romantic?"

Brian looked past Lila and smiled at Jessica. "I'm afraid I have to agree with Jessica."

Gloating, Jessica glanced at Lila, who gave her an angry glare.

"What about you, Janet?" Lila asked. Janet Howell was an eighth-grader and the president of the Unicorn Club. She also happened to be Lila's first cousin, and she almost always sided with her.

Janet looked at Brian and then at Lila. "Sorry, Lila, but I just didn't get the romance either."

Ha! I knew it! Jessica thought triumphantly. Brian was too cool for Janet to get on his wrong side.

"So is this the kind of thing you guys do on Friday nights—sit around and eat ice cream?" Brian asked. He was looking right at Jessica, and there was something teasing and flirtatious about his voice.

"What kind of stuff did you do at your old school on Friday nights?" Jessica asked, blushing.

"Well, we sure didn't eat ice cream," Brian said, chuckling.

Jessica giggled knowingly, even though she didn't really have a clue what he was talking about. "This *is* pretty boring," she admitted.

"Maybe I'll just have to liven things up a bit," Brian said, smiling.

Jessica felt a flutter of excitement in her stomach. She didn't know exactly how, but she had a feeling that with Brian around, things were going to be a lot different.

Aaron was lying in his bed on Friday night, staring at the ceiling. *I can't believe Grandpa ruined my night out with my friends,* he thought miserably. *Everyone's going to think I'm a total loser for missing the movie.*

He turned over on his stomach. He closed his eyes and imagined all his friends sitting in a booth at Casey's, laughing and talking about the movie.

This would have been a great chance for him to bond with Brian. But he knew he was better off in bed than introducing his grandfather to the gang. It wasn't just that Aaron would seem like a little kid. Aaron hated to admit it, but as much as he loved his grandfather, he was also embarrassed by him. It was his accent, his weird English, and his old-fashioned mannerisms. *He's just—different*, Aaron thought.

On Sunday evening, Aaron was stretched out comfortably on the family room couch, psyched to watch a Lakers basketball game on TV. It was a really important game, and Aaron knew everyone would be talking about it in school the next day.

As Aaron scooped up a handful of popcorn from the big bowl he'd popped especially for the game, his grandfather walked into the room. "Aaron, I have something I want to show you," he said in his thick accent. He was carrying a big, black, dusty book in his hands.

"Can you show me later?" Aaron asked, looking at the TV screen. "The game's about to start."

"What kind of game?" Mr. Kramer asked as he sat down next to Aaron on the couch.

"Basketball," Aaron mumbled distractedly.

"I love basketball," Mr. Kramer said.

Aaron glanced at his grandfather. "I didn't think they had basketball in Austria."

"Well, they don't," Mr. Kramer said. "But they have it in New Jersey, and I *have* been living there for forty years."

Aaron always forgot that his grandfather had been living in America for so long—his accent was still so strong, it seemed as if he'd just arrived.

"After my operation I watched it in my hospital room all the time," Mr. Kramer continued. "It helped pass the time."

Aaron felt a little pang of guilt. His mom told him that his grandfather had been so sick he almost died. *I'm lucky to have him here,* he thought. *I should show a little more appreciation.*

He looked at the book in his grandfather's lap. "What's in the book?"

Mr. Kramer's face lit up in a smile. "I was going through some things in the trunk your mother keeps in the attic, and I found this photo album," he said. He scooted closer to Aaron on the couch and opened the album so that it fell on top of both of their laps.

Aaron swallowed a sigh. He knew there was no way he was going to get to see the game now.

Mr. Kramer flipped over the first brittle, black page, releasing a cloud of dust into the air.

"Sheesh, how old is this thing?" Aaron asked, coughing a little and waving the dust away from the front of his face.

"This was my mother's photo album from the old days," Mr. Kramer said as he leaned forward and examined the pages carefully.

Aaron looked at the cracked, faded photos. They were dark and pretty boring-looking—just some people standing around. At the sound of cheering from the TV, he looked back up. "The Lakers have the ball!" he announced, turning up the sound with the remote control.

"This is my sister, Rachel," Mr. Kramer said. He put his hand on top of the photo lovingly and caressed it. "She was a great beauty."

"Hmmm," Aaron murmured.

"All my friends used to come over to our house just to see her," he said.

"Uh-huh," Aaron mumbled as he watched the screen.

"And she would pay them no attention." Mr. Kramer chuckled and shook his head. "She was stubborn. When she finally did agree to go to the park on a Sunday afternoon with my very best friend, Leo, Mama and Papa made me go, too. It was a good-luck thing, because they ended up getting married."

Aaron looked back down at the picture. "So where is Rachel now?" he asked.

Mr. Kramer's eyes grew misty. "She died during the war," he said almost in a whisper. "My three beautiful sisters all died, and so did my mama and papa."

Aaron bit his lip. "Oh, yeah, I forgot," he said awkwardly. He *did* know that his grandfather lost his whole family in World War Two, but he didn't know the details—and the truth was that he didn't really want to know. He didn't like hearing about sad things. "I'm sorry," he said under his breath.

"This is Sarah," Mr. Kramer continued. He was pointing to a worn photo of a girl who looked as if she was about twelve years old—Aaron's age. She had two long braids and was wearing a sailor shirt and a long skirt.

"What's that she's holding?" Aaron asked.

"That's a wooden doll she used to call Greta," Mr. Kramer said. "She took that doll with her wherever she went. Even when she was fourteen, she used to take that doll with her to the market. Finally, Mama had to take Greta away from her because she was afraid the other children would make fun of her."

Aaron heard the roar of applause from the television set and looked up to see what he had missed. Judging from the reaction of the crowds, it was something major—a missed foul shot or an interception or something.

Grandpa turned the pages of the album slowly and stopped when he came to one that had a single big photo on it. "That was our house," he said slowly.

Aaron sighed and glanced at the photo. From what he could see, it didn't look like much of a house. It was pretty small, especially compared with the houses in Sweet Valley, and there wasn't a yard or anything in the front of it.

"That's nice," Aaron said, trying to sound interested.

"It was a very special house," Mr. Kramer said sadly. "We had to leave when the Nazis came."

Aaron squirmed in his seat. *Nazis*. That word made him shiver. He knew that the Nazis had come to Austria in World War Two and that they were the reason his grandfather had lost his family. But Aaron didn't like thinking about that stuff.

"It looks like the Lakers are going to win this thing," Aaron said, trying to change the subject.

"It was a very special house," Mr. Kramer repeated in a whisper.

Three

"Hey, Aaron, we missed you on Friday," Brian said on Monday morning as he walked up to Aaron's locker with Ken Matthews. "You're not afraid of a little horror movie or anything, are you?"

"Yeah, Dallas, what happened to you?" Ken asked. "I thought we had a set plan."

Aaron shut the door of his locker and turned to face Brian, who wore a teasing grin on his face. "Oh, I should have called you," he said, trying to sound casual. "I came down with some kind of stomach thing. It was pretty wicked."

"Really?" Ken asked. "You sounded OK when I talked to you just before I left."

"Yeah, well, it was one of those sudden-attack viruses," Aaron said quickly. "One minute you're fine, and the next—wham!"

"I guess it's just as well you didn't come," Brian said, smiling. "Otherwise you might have been hurling all over us in the movie."

Aaron laughed along with Ken and Brian. He felt relieved that he didn't have to explain his absence any further. "So did you guys have a good time?" he asked.

"It was OK," Brian said. "The movie was pretty cool, and there were some hot girls at that ice cream place afterwards."

"Yeah? Like who?" Aaron asked.

Brian gave Aaron a knowing grin and a wink. "Well, like Jessica Wakefield, for instance. I hear you guys kind of have a thing going."

Jessica and Aaron *were* sort of girlfriend and boyfriend. Basically, they danced together whenever there was a boy-girl party, and they talked on the phone every now and then. It seemed weird that Brian was kind of bonding with him over Jessica—but in a way, it made Aaron feel really important.

"You could say that," Aaron said.

"You're a lucky man," Brian told him, looking at him meaningfully.

"Yeah, I guess so," Aaron said, smiling. "She's a great girl."

"So who caught the Lakers game last night?" Ken asked.

"I was supposed to go to the game, but my tickets fell through at the last minute," Brian said. "I had to watch it on TV. It's so much better to watch it live."

"That's so cool," Ken said. "I've never been to a live Lakers game."

"Really? You're kidding." Brian sounded as though he'd never heard of such a thing. "What about you, Aaron?"

"Actually, I've been to a lot of them," Aaron said before he knew what he was saying. In fact, he'd only been to one game before. He didn't lie very often, but for some reason, he couldn't resist the idea of impressing Brian. He could tell that Brian had really set ideas about what was cool and what wasn't—and something told Aaron that it was best to be on Brian's good side.

Ken looked at Aaron doubtfully. "You never mentioned going to a lot of Lakers games before."

"I just didn't want to show off, I guess," Aaron said nonchalantly.

"What's the last game you went to?" Brian asked.

"Oh, I went last night," Aaron said, amazed at how the lie was growing.

"That's awesome," Brian said, obviously impressed. "It was a great game."

"Yeah, you should have been there. The crowd went crazy when they scored that final point in overtime," Aaron said, his face heating up.

"Maybe you could get tickets for all of us sometime," Brian said.

"Sure, no problem," Aaron said, even though he knew he had about as much a chance of getting tickets as he did of going to the moon.

* * *

"Jessica, wake up," Elizabeth whispered urgently on Monday morning as social studies class was about to start. "Here comes Mrs. Arnette."

Jessica slowly opened her eyes and looked at her sister. She wasn't really going to sleep, just resting a little. She was preparing herself for another boring class.

"Can't you just wake me when it's over?" Jessica asked, yawning. "Hairnet hasn't even started talking yet, and I'm already bored out of my mind."

Hairnet was the students' name for Mrs. Arnette, since she wore a hairnet over her gray bun every day. She was one of Jessica's least favorite teachers—she was always getting mad at her for whispering and sending notes to her friends in class. But Jessica *had* to send notes. How else was she supposed to stay awake?

"Who's that man standing up there?" Elizabeth whispered.

Jessica's eyes widened as she looked toward the front of the class. Suddenly, she sat straight up in her chair. Standing next to Hairnet was a man with brown curly hair. He was wearing a gray tweed jacket with a blue oxford shirt, and he had on round, wire-framed glasses.

"I don't know who he is, but he's totally adorable," Jessica whispered excitedly. "He looks like he's about twenty-eight or something."

"OK, class," Mrs. Arnette called out over the

whispers and the sounds of chairs scraping against the floor. "If I may have your undivided attention, please."

"The only thing getting attention from me in this room is that total hunk," Jessica whispered to Elizabeth.

"Shhhh," Elizabeth warned.

"I want to introduce a special visitor today," Mrs. Arnette said. "This is Barry Levin, and he's going to be with us for the next couple of weeks to help us prepare for our studies of World War Two."

"Good morning," Mr. Levin said, smiling broadly.

"Good morning!" Jessica said loudly. She looked around the room and realized she was the only student who had replied to his greeting.

"Looks like Jessica has a crush," Veronica Brooks whispered loudly behind her.

Jessica shot her a glare. Veronica was one of Jessica's least favorite people in the whole school. Not only had she tried to frame Jessica for stealing, but she had also tried to break up Jessica and Aaron.

"Mind your own business," Jessica hissed to Veronica before turning back to face Mr. Levin.

"How many of you have heard the word *Holocaust*?" Mr. Levin asked.

More than half the class, including Jessica and Elizabeth, raised their hands.

"Good," Mr. Levin said. "How many of you know what happened during the Holocaust of World War Two?"

Jessica sort of knew what happened, although she couldn't really give an exact answer. She knew it had something to do with a horrible man in Germany named Hitler who killed people because they were Jewish, but that was about it. She looked around the room and saw that only a few people had raised their hands.

"Well, in the next couple of weeks we're going to learn all about the Holocaust," Mr. Levin continued. "And we're going to start by playing a game. Soon, you'll see that you're not only playing a game, you're learning a history lesson as well."

"So what kind of game is it?" Brian called out. "Get to the point."

Jessica let out a small gasp. *That's a pretty nervy way to talk to a teacher,* she thought, both shocked and impressed.

Mr. Levin raised an eyebrow, but he didn't really look offended or irritated by Brian's rudeness—he seemed almost amused.

"I don't know how the students at your old school talked to teachers," Mrs. Arnette addressed Brian sternly, "but here at Sweet Valley Middle School, students are expected to treat their teachers with respect. I want you to apologize to Mr. Levin."

"Sorry," Brian said under his breath with a big grin on his face.

"What's your name?" Mr. Levin asked.

"Brian Boyd," he answered, crossing his arms in front of his body.

"And you're new to Sweet Valley Middle School?" Mr. Levin asked.

"Yep," Brian replied.

"How long have you been here?"

Brian let out a deep, impatient breath. "One week," he said flatly.

Mr. Levin wrote something down in his notebook, then looked around the room. "OK, the first part of the game is going to be about following directions. Tomorrow, I want everyone here to wear a white shirt. If anyone doesn't have one, I have some extras here that I can lend you."

"What does that have to do with the Holocaust?" Veronica asked.

"You'll see as we go along," Mr. Levin replied simply.

Elizabeth furrowed her brow. "This seems like a pretty weird assignment," she whispered to Jessica.

"Hmmm," Jessica responded. She was already wondering which white shirt she was going to wear—the cotton one with the ruffles or her silk one with the French cuffs.

"Is that it?" Brian asked. "Is that the game?"

"That's the first part of the game," Mr. Levin said. "I want to see how good you all are at following directions. And remember, this is an assignment—if you fail to follow the directions, I'll have to downgrade you. And if you catch anyone in this class who, over the course of the day, isn't wearing a white shirt as assigned, you can receive extra points by reporting it to me."

Elizabeth frowned. "That's the craziest thing I ever heard," she said to Jessica as the bell rang.

"Oh, come on, Lizzie. You should be good at this game," Jessica responded.

"Why's that?" Elizabeth asked.

"Because all you ever do is follow directions," Jessica said. "In fact, you're so good at doing what you're supposed to do that you forget to have any fun."

"That's not true," Elizabeth protested.

"Is too," Jessica teased.

"Is not!"

Jessica walked into social studies class on Tuesday morning feeling more excited about school than she had in a long time. Even though she didn't really see the point of it, the game they were playing seemed really fun. She had decided to wear her ruffly white shirt, and she loved getting dressed up for an assignment.

She sat down next to Elizabeth and looked around the room. Everyone was wearing a white shirt!

"Something about this assignment is giving me the creeps," Elizabeth said to Jessica. "I feel like we're in a military school or something."

Jessica made a horrified face. "Don't even *joke* about something like that, Elizabeth. Can you imagine if we *did* have to wear some military-looking uniform every day? I'd have nothing to live for."

Elizabeth grinned. "Yeah, that would be pretty tragic," she teased. "What would you and your friends talk about if you couldn't talk about clothes?"

Mr. Levin wrapped on the desk to get the class's attention. "Good morning," he said to the class. "I see you all followed your directions perfectly. You'll all receive high marks."

"Well, it wasn't the most difficult assignment in the world," Brian joked.

"You're right," Mr. Levin agreed. "We started out with something very simple. It was just an example to start you off on the real part of the game."

"I can hardly wait to see what's next," Brian said, smiling. "Do we get to move on to wearing blue or something?" He looked around at the class, his eyes sparkling.

Jessica couldn't help giggling, along with a lot of other kids. There was something really exciting about hearing Brian talk back to the teacher. He wasn't just a normal obnoxious loudmouth, and he wasn't just showing off—it seemed as though he really wanted people to laugh along *with* him.

When Brian's eyes met Jessica's, he winked. Jessica blushed—she felt as though she were included in some really great inside joke.

Even Mr. Levin was smiling. "Brian, please come to the front of the class," he instructed.

Brian raised his eyebrows in surprise, then stood up and walked coolly to the front of the room, then folded his arms in a casual pose.

"Brian, you're going to be a key player in the game," Mr. Levin said.

"Awesome," Brian said, smiling confidently.

Mr. Levin scanned the class for a few moments.

"And what's your name?" Mr. Levin asked, pointing to Brooke Dennis.

Brooke cleared her throat. "Brooke Dennis," she said timidly.

"Brooke, could you come stand up here next to Brian?" Mr. Levin requested.

Reluctantly, Brooke walked up and stood next to Brian.

"Mrs. Arnette, how many people are in this class?" Mr. Levin asked.

"Twenty-four," Mrs. Arnette replied.

"OK, Brian," Mr. Levin began. He sat down on top of Mrs. Arnette's desk and crossed his legs. "I want you to choose eleven people and have them all stand against the wall on the right."

Brian scrunched up his face as if sun were shining right in his eyes. "What for? Is this for some kind of sports thing or something?"

"You'll see once we get started. For now, just choose people randomly," Mr. Levin instructed.

Brian shook his head as if that was the dumbest thing he'd ever heard of, then looked around the room.

"Uh . . . OK, Aaron Dallas, Ken Matthews, the Wakefield girls . . ." Brian began. He smiled at the twins mischievously.

Elizabeth shot Jessica a look as they stood up. "Do you see how he's staring at us? I think it's creepy," she whispered.

Jessica was staring straight back at Brian, smiling brightly. "Lighten up, Elizabeth. He thinks we're cute. Can't you take a compliment?"

This is totally cool, Jessica thought as she and Elizabeth joined the others against the wall. *It's like we're being chosen for a club or something.*

As Brian continued listing names, Jessica became more and more excited. He was choosing all the coolest kids, including the Unicorns who were in the class—Lila and Mandy Miller.

"OK, I want everyone whom Brian didn't choose to go stand against the opposite wall," Mr. Levin said once Brian had selected eleven people.

As instructed, the remaining students lined up on the opposite wall.

"What we have here are two groups of people," Mr. Levin continued. "We have Brian's group and Brooke's group."

Jessica looked at the people standing on the opposite side of the room. Brooke's group included Amy Sutton and Maria Slater, two of Elizabeth's boring friends, and Winston Egbert, the biggest science nerd in the school. *Yep. The people in Brooke's group are definite losers,* Jessica thought, feeling pleased with the side of the room she was on.

"So are we going to all go play basketball now or something?" Brian joked.

Jessica and Lila snickered.

"That's up to you," Mr. Levin said flatly.

Brian raised an eyebrow. "How's that?"

"As the leader of your team, you're going to make up the rules that everyone has to follow," Mr. Levin explained.

Brian frowned. "What kind of rules?"

"This is your group, and you can do whatever you want to with them," Mr. Levin said. "The rules can be about what to wear, what to do, or what not to do. One more thing: If you decide someone can't be in your group anymore, then they're out." He turned to Brooke. "And the same goes for you. You're in charge of your group, so you can make up your own rules."

"This sounds pretty awesome," Brian said, a huge smile spreading across his face. "When do we start?"

"Right now," Mr. Levin said. "Say what your first rule is."

Brian narrowed his eyes thoughtfully. "OK, starting tomorrow, everyone has to wear a black T-shirt every day."

"And what about you, Brooke?" Mr. Levin asked. "What is your first rule going to be?"

Brooke looked flustered. "Can I think about it and make it up later?" she asked.

"Sure thing," Mr. Levin said. "From here on out, you two are in charge."

Four

I can't believe he picked me first, Aaron thought excitedly as he walked to the table where Brian was sitting in the cafeteria on Tuesday. He'd been a little worried that Brian might not be so crazy about him after he missed the movie on Friday night. But obviously Brian thought he was cool enough to be in his group.

"Hey, man," Brian said to Aaron, "I have a favor to ask you."

Aaron put his tray down on the table and took a seat. "Sure thing. What's up?"

"Well, I want you to kind of be my Special Assistant with this whole club stuff," Brian explained.

Aaron broke into an enormous grin. "Really? That's awesome." *Club,* he repeated to himself. *Special Assistant*. He liked the sound of those words.

"The thing is," Brian continued blandly, "I just

picked those people kind of randomly, and I don't know their backgrounds or anything. You've known them for a long time, right?"

"Yeah, I even went to elementary school with some of them," Aaron said eagerly.

"Good," Brian said thoughtfully. "Very good. I figured you could help me learn some stuff about people."

"Definitely," Aaron agreed, flattered that Brian considered him an authority on the kids in their group. "What kind of stuff do you want to know about them?"

"I don't know yet," Brian said as he took a big bite of lasagna. "But I will as we go along."

"I can't wait until the first club meeting," Jessica said excitedly to Mandy and Lila at lunch on Tuesday. They were sitting at the Unicorner, the table in the cafeteria where the Unicorns always sat.

"What club meeting?" Janet Howell asked sharply, just as she approached the table with her lunch tray.

Whoops—bad timing, Jessica thought. *Janet isn't going to like the idea of a new cool club in school that she's not a member of. And I don't want to be the person to tell her about it.*

"Lila, why don't you tell Janet about Brian's club?" Jessica said.

Lila shot Jessica an annoyed glare. "Actually, Mandy, I think you could explain it better."

Mandy went a little pale and shrugged sheepishly.

Janet pursed her lips. "Explain *what*?" she demanded. "Brian Boyd has a club? What kind of club?"

Jessica was waiting for Lila and Mandy to open their mouths, but they were both looking at her blankly.

"What *kind* of club, Jessica?" Janet prompted. "As your president, I need to know if there are any secret clubs being formed behind my back."

"It's not that!" Jessica insisted.

"What *is* it, then?" Janet asked, gritting her teeth.

Jessica took a deep breath. *I guess I better get this over with.* "Look, it's not really any big deal," she reassured Janet. "It's a school project kind of thing."

"Get to the point," Janet said, rolling her big brown eyes.

"Well, Mr. Levin, this visiting teacher in our social studies class, came up with this game for our class to play," Jessica said quickly.

"Uh-huh . . . and?" Janet said impatiently.

"And anyway, he told Brian to choose up half the class to be in his group, and Brooke Dennis got stuck with the rest of the class," Jessica explained.

"Brian chose all three of us to be in his group," Mandy blurted out.

"Who else was chosen to be in his group?" Janet asked.

Jessica listed the people in Brian's group, and Janet furrowed her brow.

"So he obviously has the popular group of people," Janet concluded.

"Yeah, I guess it looks like that," Jessica confirmed, smiling a little to herself.

"And what exactly is your group supposed to do?" Janet asked.

"We don't know yet," Lila said. "Our first meeting is this afternoon."

"Basically, Mr. Levin said that Brian can make up the rules," Jessica explained. "And he can decide who he wants to stay in his group."

Janet looked thoughtful. "So if, say, he decides that there's someone who's really cool who's *not* in the group, he can expand his group to include that person."

Jessica, Lila, and Mandy looked at one another.

"What do you mean?" Mandy asked.

"Let me put it to you this way," Janet said. "Brian probably wants this to be the coolest club possible, right?"

Jessica nodded.

"Well, then he should have seventh- and eighth-graders as well," Janet announced briskly. "And the three of you can suggest that to him this afternoon."

"Hmmmm." Jessica reflected for a moment. She wasn't exactly sure how open to suggestions Brian was. On the other hand, Janet had a point—the club would be a lot cooler with older kids in it. And the more she thought about it, the more she figured Brian would agree. *And if I'm the one who suggests it to him, he'll really think I'm OK.*

"Great idea," Jessica said excitedly. "I'll mention it to him this afternoon."

Aaron was practically out of breath as he raced down the front steps of the school. Brian's first club meeting was supposed to be in the parking lot of Casey's in a half hour, but Aaron was so psyched for it, he wanted to get there early. He was wearing a black T-shirt that was a little too big for him, but he didn't care—dressing for the game was really fun and exciting.

"Aaron!"

Aaron spun around to see his grandfather standing at the entrance to the path from the street.

"Grandpa!" Aaron exclaimed, joining him by the entrance. "What are you doing here?"

"I came to walk you home," Mr. Kramer said, beaming.

"Oh. I mean, that's nice of you, but, um, aren't you supposed to be at home resting?" Aaron glanced over his shoulder to see if anybody was looking. *If anybody catches me walking home with my grandfather, I'll look like a little kid.*

Mr. Kramer shook his head. "My doctor told me to walk every day," he explained. "He said it was the best thing I could do for my heart."

Aaron felt a pang of affection for his grandfather. He really wanted to get to the meeting, but he couldn't exactly tell his grandfather to walk home alone. "Listen, Grandpa," he said, "I have this important meeting I have to go to, so I just have time to walk with you partway, all right?"

"That would be very good," Mr. Kramer said as they started walking down the street together. "Where do you have to be?"

"I'm going to a meeting for a new club I just became a member of," Aaron explained.

"What kind of club?"

Aaron shrugged. "I'm not exactly sure. But I know it's the club to be in, because it's made up of really cool people." Aaron felt a surge of excitement just talking about the club.

"And what of the people who are not in this club?" Mr. Kramer asked. "What happens to them?"

"Uh . . . well, they're in another club," Aaron said. "It's not as good as the one that I'm in, but it's still a club."

"And why is yours so good?" Mr. Kramer pressed.

Aaron smiled to himself. It was funny how curious his grandfather was about Aaron's life and activities and everything. "Well, this great guy named Brian Boyd is the leader of it," Aaron explained. "He just moved here from Los Angeles, and he's already really popular at school."

"And this is a nice person, this Brian Boyd?" Grandpa asked.

Nice wasn't exactly the word that came to mind when Aaron thought about Brian, but he knew he couldn't explain why he was so cool to his grandfather—he wouldn't really get it. "Sure, he's a nice guy," he answered.

"And you say you don't know exactly what kind of club it is? You don't know what kind of activities you do in this club?"

Why is Grandpa giving me the third degree? Aaron wondered as he looked as his watch.

"Whoa—it's later than I thought," Aaron said quickly. "I better get going if I want to be on time."

"OK, you go," Mr. Kramer instructed. "But Aaron?"

Aaron had already started walking away. "Yeah?" he asked, turning around.

"I want you to promise me one thing," Mr. Kramer said.

"What?" Aaron asked, trying not to sound impatient.

"Be careful about this club," Mr. Kramer warned.

"What's there to be careful about?" Aaron asked.

"Just be careful," he repeated. "Clubs can be dangerous things."

"Yeah, sure, I'll be careful," Aaron said, then bounded off toward Casey's. *Grandpa is really getting weird in his old age,* he thought. *He's such a downer!*

Five

"Hey, Jessica, did I miss anything?" Aaron asked breathlessly as he arrived at the club meeting. All the kids Brian chose to be in his group were sitting in a circle on the grassy field next to Casey's parking lot. Everyone was wearing some kind of black T-shirt. Brian was standing in the middle, wearing his black leather jacket.

"No, you're just in time," Jessica told him.

As Aaron sat down next to Jessica, he noticed that she looked prettier than ever. The front part of her long hair was pulled back in a barrette and she was wearing a pretty pink sweater over her black T-shirt.

"So Brian's just been standing there the whole time?" Aaron whispered to Jessica.

"Hmm?" she mumbled.

"I said has Brian—" Aaron glanced at Jessica and saw that she was completely focused on Brian. She probably hadn't heard a word he said. *That's OK,* Aaron reasoned. *I mean, Brian's a pretty cool guy—it's no wonder she's paying attention to him. She'll be impressed when she sees how tight the two of us are getting.*

"Could everyone pipe down?" Brian commanded, as he stood in front of his chosen group of people. "The meeting is about to begin."

Silence fell around the circle, and all faces were turned eagerly up toward their leader.

"I'm glad you're all wearing black T-shirts, as instructed," Brian said, sounding pleased, as he looked around the circle. His eyes rested on Aaron. "Aaron, could you write down the names of everyone who's here and everyone who's not here?"

"Sure, no problem," Aaron replied promptly, thrilled that Brian was giving him so much responsibility in the group. He quickly pulled a notebook and a pen out of his knapsack and looked around the circle.

"Now, I want to talk a little bit about what's going to be expected of all of you," Brian said as he paced back and forth in the center of the circle. "We are going to have the reputation for being the coolest group of people in the school, and we all have to live up to that. You're expected to dress in only the hippest kind of clothes and listen to the hottest new music."

"Wow! It's just like the Unicorns, only bigger!" Jessica exclaimed in a whisper. "And including guys!"

Aaron smiled. In his opinion, the club was already seeming way cooler than the Unicorns—it just seemed more important and powerful somehow.

"For this reason," Brian continued, "I've come up with the perfect name for our club—*IN*."

"That's really great," Jake Hamilton said enthusiastically. "*In* like as opposed to *Out*."

"Exactly," Brian said. "Everyone who's not *IN* will want to be. Those of you who are privileged enough to be *IN* should be careful not to lose your membership."

"What sort of things will make us lose our membership?" Elizabeth asked.

Aaron was actually wondering the same thing but was a little embarrassed to ask.

"That will just be left to me to decide," Brian said. "But keep in mind that just because you're here right now doesn't mean you should assume that you're definitely in the club for good." He looked around the circle slowly, his eyes falling heavily on each of the members of *IN*. "No one should take membership for granted. I'm still getting to know all of you."

"How are we supposed to know if we've done something wrong?" Aaron heard Ken Matthews whisper.

"I guess we'll just have to be extra-careful not to

do anything that's uncool," Lila whispered back.

"Any other questions?" Brian asked over the whispers.

Jessica raised her hand. "I was wondering if you're considering opening the group up to people outside of our class," she asked. "Like, maybe let seventh- and eighth-graders in, too?"

Brian rubbed his chin with his fingers. "I think that's a good idea—it would make us even more desirable. And since Mr. Levin said it's up to me to decide who should be in the club, I think I'll consider some *qualified* seventh- and eighth-graders."

"If you want I could give you a list of some seventh- and eighth-graders who are interested in joining," Jessica offered.

"No, I think it's better if I just observe people myself," Brian said. "The requirements for being *IN* material are very . . . complex. I'll have to make my selection after careful consideration."

"Oh. Right," Jessica said, blushing slightly.

Melissa McCormick raised her hand. "If the group is open to people outside our class, how will we know who's a member and who isn't?"

"I was just getting to that," Brian said. "Does anyone have any suggestions?"

"How about if we all wear bandannas around our necks?" Aaron suggested.

Brian looked at Aaron and narrowed his eyes as if he were concentrating deeply. "Not bad," he said. "Anyone else?"

Lila waved her hand around in the air wildly. "As you probably know," she began, "Jessica, Mandy, and I are all members of the Unicorn club."

"Yes, I know that," Brian said, folding his arms.

"Well, every day we all try to wear one purple article of clothing or accessory as a sign of our membership," she explained.

Brian stared at her blankly. "Uh-huh."

"I was thinking that maybe all the members of *IN* could do the same kind of thing—like wear a piece of clothing or something every day but in another color," Lila suggested.

Brian shook his head. "That's too vague. It's not a solid enough statement. Anyone else?"

"Armbands?" Jessica suggested.

Brian smiled. "I like it. Every day, all members of *IN* will wear a black armband, but you also have to wear the black T-shirts, like I already told you."

"What kind of activities will we be doing?" Mandy asked.

"Activities?" Brian asked, as if he'd never heard the word before. "That sounds like what you do after you have milk and cookies in kindergarten."

Everyone laughed. Mandy's face turned bright pink.

"The only activity we'll be doing is hanging," Brian said. "Like hanging at the mall together and stuff."

"Cool!" Jessica exclaimed. "I love the mall!"

"And every now and then there will be little

tests people will have to do to secure their membership," Brian said.

"What kind of tests?" Elizabeth asked.

Brian stared hard at Elizabeth. "You'll just have to wait and find out," he replied.

"That new club you're in sounds really cool," Randy Mason said to Aaron on Tuesday night. They were sitting in Aaron's family room, doing homework together.

Aaron glanced at his friend. "I didn't know you were so into clubs and stuff," he said. He thought Randy was a great guy, but he didn't really have the coolest interests.

"Yeah, well, this club is different," Randy responded. "The whole school's really excited about it."

Aaron smiled proudly. "Yeah, I guess you're right."

"Anyway," Randy continued, "I heard that Brian's opening it up to people who aren't in your social studies class."

"Yeah, anyone can be a member," Aaron confirmed.

"So, do you think I could be one?" Randy asked eagerly, pushing aside his math book.

Aaron hesitated. Something told him that Randy wasn't exactly Brian's kind of person—he was into science and that sort of thing. On the other hand, Brian seemed to really value Aaron's opinion. *As his Special Assistant, I could probably convince Brian that Randy is perfect* IN *material,* he thought confidently.

"I don't see why not," Aaron told Randy. "Brian and I have been getting pretty friendly lately."

"Could you put in a good word for me?" Randy asked.

"Sure thing," Aaron said, feeling proud of the power he had.

"What's he basing membership on, anyway?" Randy asked.

Aaron shrugged. "I don't really know," he admitted.

Randy looked at Aaron uncertainly. "So how do I know what I have to do to be a member? I mean, I'm sure your recommendation will help and everything, but—"

"Hey, any friend of mine will be a friend of Brian's," Aaron broke in reassuringly.

"Hello, Aaron," Mr. Kramer said as he suddenly appeared in the room. "Who is this nice young man?"

Randy stood up and walked across the room, extending his hand. "I'm Randy Mason," he said politely. "You must be Mr. Kramer."

Mr. Kramer sat down in one of the comfortable chairs next to the couch. "Yes, but you can call me Grandpa," he said.

Aaron felt a twinge of embarrassment. Even though Randy was too nice a guy to laugh at his grandfather, Aaron thought it would be best to clear out of the old man's way as soon as possible. He didn't want Randy thinking his family was really weird.

"You look a litte tired, Grandpa," Aaron said, jumping up from the couch. "Randy and I will get out of your way. We can finish studying in my room."

"You're not in my way at all," Mr. Kramer argued jovially. "I just woke up from a nap."

"Actually, I'm in no great hurry to hit the books again. I'd like to stay and visit with Grandpa for a little while," Randy said.

"Well, if you say so," Aaron said hesitantly.

Randy was leaning forward, smiling pleasantly at Mr. Kramer. "So where are you from, Grandpa?"

"I come from Vienna, Austria," Mr. Kramer said with a smile. "Do you know where that is?"

"Of course," Randy answered. "My grandparents were from there."

Mr. Kramer looked absolutely overjoyed. "What are their names?"

"Their names were Laura and Samuel Jacobs," Randy said, then he looked down at the carpet. "But they're both dead now."

"I'm sorry to hear it, my boy," Mr. Kramer said affectionately. "I did use to play with a David Jacobs. Could he be one of your relatives?"

Randy shook his head. "I don't know any David Jacobs." He smiled. "So tell me about Vienna."

"It was a beautiful, magical city," Mr. Kramer began.

Aaron shuffled his feet restlessly. He knew that once his grandfather got started on Vienna, they could be there all night. "Listen, I have a lot of homework, Grandpa. We should really get going."

Mr. Kramer nodded and smiled. "Randy, maybe you'll come back sometime soon, and I'll tell you some stories about Vienna."

"I'd like that," Randy said with a grin.

"And I'll even show you some magic tricks," Mr. Kramer continued. "Aaron loves my magic tricks. Don't you?"

Aaron shifted his weight from one leg to the other. "Yeah, I love them, Grandpa," he said.

"Sorry about Grandpa," Aaron said when he and Randy were standing on the front steps of Aaron's house.

Randy raised his eyebrows in surprise. "What are you sorry about?"

"You know," Aaron began. "How he came in and bothered us while we were studying and talking and stuff."

"It wasn't any bother," Randy said. "He seems like a really cool guy."

"Well, yeah, he is really cool," Aaron admitted, feeling a little confused. On the one hand, he *did* think his grandfather was a great guy—really sweet and funny and everything. But on the other hand, he just seemed so strange and old-fashioned, always talking about stuff that was so far off and long ago.

"You're lucky to have him around," Randy went on. "My grandfather died last year and I miss him every day."

"I'm sorry," Aaron said softly. "That must be rough."

"Actually, your grandfather reminds me of him," Randy added. "He has the same accent as my grandfather did."

"Really?" Aaron asked. "Did your grandfather go on and on about people who are dead and about the old days?"

Randy laughed. "All the time," he said fondly. "You can really learn a lot from them."

"Yeah, I guess so," Aaron said, though in fact he wasn't at all sure what he could learn from old, faded photographs and stories about some pretty city practically on the other side of the world. "Well, I guess I'll see you tomorrow, then."

"You bet," Randy said, as he started down the stairs. "Oh, Aaron—one more thing."

"Uh-huh?"

"Don't forget to mention to Brian about me being in the club," Randy said.

"You got it," Aaron said. "No problem."

Six

"Hey, Earth to Jessica," Steven Wakefield, Elizabeth and Jessica's older brother, teased. "Pass the fish sticks."

The Wakefields were eating dinner in the kitchen on Tuesday night and Jessica had one thing on her mind—Brian's club.

Jessica handed Steven the platter and turned to Elizabeth. "I have to say, I've never had such a blast doing a social studies assignment in my life. If we could do stuff like this in all our classes, I'd be the best student in school."

Elizabeth rolled her eyes. "If we had to do this in all our classes, I'd probably drop out," she said, pouring ketchup on her fish sticks. "All those rules about what music to listen to and what kinds of clothes to wear—" She broke off, shaking her head. "I don't need someone telling me how to live my life."

Jessica looked at her in amazement. "I can't believe that you, of all people, would complain about following rules. I mean, you're the most rule-following person in America."

"Well, I don't need to follow *his* rules," Elizabeth said firmly.

"Oh, come on, Lizzie. There's nothing wrong with following *fun* rules for a change. Besides, if you don't get a more positive attitude about the club, Brian will get mad at you," Jessica warned.

Elizabeth sighed. "Ask me how much I care if he does get mad."

"Elizabeth, why do you have to be the most stubborn—"

"Wait a minute," Mr. Wakefield interrupted. "Back up, you two. What assignment are you talking about?"

"Actually, can we not use the word *assignment* while we're eating?" Jessica asked. "In this case, it's not really appropriate. What we're talking about here is this cool new club that started at school."

Steven gasped dramatically. "Don't tell me the Unicorns have disbanded! What will happen to Sweet Valley without them?"

Jessica stuck her tongue out at her brother. He was always teasing her about the Unicorns, who he thought were incredibly silly. Whenever she had a Unicorn meeting at the house, Steven threw a fit.

"Don't worry, brother dear," Jessica said sarcastically. "The Unicorns are alive and well, and in fact, you can see all of them tomorrow."

Steven frowned. "I can?"

"Yes. There's going to be a meeting right here at four o'clock," Jessica said.

"Remind me to get a ticket for Mexico," Steven groaned.

"Can you continue telling us about this new assignment or club or whatever it is?" Mrs. Wakefield asked as she poured iced tea into everyone's glass.

"Actually it did start out as an assignment for social studies class," Elizabeth began before Jessica could say another word. "This visiting teacher, Mr. Levin, divided the class into two groups."

"What kind of groups?" Mr. Wakefield asked.

"That's the weird thing," Elizabeth said. "He appointed two different leaders and told them to make up whatever kind of rules they wanted—what to wear, who will be a member, that type of thing."

"And this guy, Brian, who's leading our group, is totally hip and cool," Jessica added.

"According to some people," Elizabeth amended.

"It doesn't sound as if you think he's so great," Mrs. Wakefield said to Elizabeth.

"I actually don't know him all that well, but he kind of gives me the creeps," Elizabeth said.

"You shouldn't make judgments about people before you know them," Jessica pointed out.

"I just don't have a good feeling about him," Elizabeth argued.

"I don't understand why this is a social studies project," Mr. Wakefield interrupted. "I think I'm missing something here."

"That's the part I don't get either," Elizabeth said. "It's supposed to be an introduction to the Holocaust."

Mr. and Mrs. Wakefield looked at each other as if they understood. "I see," Mr. Wakefield said. "I'll be curious to know how this all turns out."

"Tell me about Bruce Patman," Brian said to Aaron at the lunch table on Wednesday. "He seems like a good candidate for the club."

Aaron looked across the cafeteria to where Bruce was laughing and talking loudly with Rick Hunter. "Well, he's a seventh-grader and he's the richest guy in the school," Aaron began. "He's also kind of on the obnoxious side."

"Yeah? How's that?" Brian asked.

"He's just a real show-off," Aaron explained. "And he makes fun of people who he doesn't think are cool. That kind of thing."

"I want him at the next meeting," Brian said. "Make sure he's there."

Aaron looked across the table at Brian. "You got it," he said even though he was a little surprised. *That wasn't exactly a glowing recommendation I just gave.*

"Hey, guys," Randy said as he walked up to their table with his lunch tray and sat down. "How's it going?"

Shoot. I forgot to mention to Brian about Randy wanting to be in the club, Aaron realized. *Oh, well. Maybe this will be a good time for Brian to get to know him.*

"Hi, Randy," Aaron said. "Have you met Brian yet?"

"Yeah, we met last week," Randy said cheerfully. "How are you liking Sweet Valley so far?"

"It's OK," Brian said unexcitedly.

"Hey, maybe I can show you around sometime," Randy said as he started to sit down at the table.

Brian looked up at Randy blankly. "Sorry, man, but that seat's taken," he said flatly. "Jake Hamilton is sitting there."

Aaron almost spat out the sip of milk in his mouth. *What's he talking about?* he wondered. Jake was sitting at a table on the other side of the room.

Randy's lip trembled just a bit as he stood up. "Oh . . . uh . . . I didn't know," he said quietly. "I'll see you guys around."

Randy quickly walked away from the table before Aaron could say a word.

"I'm surprised you're not sitting with Brian and the rest of your new club," Maria Slater said to Elizabeth in the cafeteria on Wednesday.

"Yeah, really," Amy Sutton agreed. "You might

get on Brian's bad side if he sees you sitting with us. I thought that was one of his new rules."

"It is one of his rules, but I'm just going to have to break it," Elizabeth said. "It's bad enough that I'm wearing this stupid black T-shirt. I missed you guys too much when I was in seventh grade for those couple of weeks. I'm not going to let this new club keep us apart."

"Well, we don't want to get you in trouble with Brian," Amy said. "I heard that he wasn't very nice to his enemies at his old school."

Elizabeth frowned. "Where'd you hear that?"

"My cousin, Emily, goes to his old school in Los Angeles," Amy explained. "She said Brian was the most popular guy there, and he made you feel great if he liked you. But she said not to get on his bad side."

"Did she say anything more specific?" Elizabeth asked.

Amy shook her head. "No, that was it."

"Well, I'll take my chances," Elizabeth said. "Some kids might feel great that he likes them, but I could really care less."

"But aren't you the tiniest bit flattered that he chose you to be in his group?" Maria asked. "I mean, Brian obviously chose the kids he thought were the coolest, and it sounds like you'll be a pretty big force in the school. So far, our group hasn't done anything too exciting at all."

"You sound like Jessica," Elizabeth said, smiling.

"Both of you are too great to worry about being in a silly club."

"That's easy for you to say when you're in Brian's group," Maria pointed out.

"Believe me, the only good thing about being in Brian's group is that I'll be able to keep tabs on what he's doing," Elizabeth said. "I can't put my finger on it, but there's something fishy about that guy."

"So you're planning on doing some detective work, are you?" Maria teased.

"You might say that," Elizabeth said, her eyes sparkling. "You know how I love a good mystery."

"Thanks for talking to Brian about expanding the club," Janet said to Jessica on Wednesday afternoon. "I got a call from Aaron last night to come to the next meeting on Thursday."

The girls were sitting on the floor of Jessica's bedroom with the other Unicorns, having a meeting. They all had green clay masks on their faces, and they were waiting for them to dry.

"Don't mention it," Jessica said. "I hope you'll be chosen as a member."

Janet looked at Jessica as though she were from Mars. "What do you mean, you *hope* I'll be chosen? Can you think of a *better* candidate to be a member of the new cool club in school?"

"Oh. Right. I mean, no," Jessica corrected, flustered. Even though Jessica totally looked up to

Janet, she sometimes thought she was just a little too conceited.

"Guess what? I was invited to the meeting, too," Tamara said.

"So was I," Mary Wallace added.

Ellen let out a heavy sigh. "So I guess all the Unicorns have been invited except for me."

For a moment silence fell over the group.

"Don't worry," Lila said finally. "I'm sure it was just a mistake."

"I hope you're right," Ellen said. "It would be way too humiliating to be the only Unicorn not in *IN*."

Just then the door to Jessica's room flung open, and Steven appeared in the doorway, clutching a camera, a devilish grin on his face.

"Yikes!" Lila shrieked as she covered up her face.

"Get him out of here!" Janet yelled as she bent her head over her knees.

"Steven, get out of my room this minute!" Jessica commanded. "Say green cheese," Steven said, as he clicked the button on his camera.

"This is an awesome house," Aaron said to Brian on Wednesday afternoon, as he followed him into the front hallway of his house. "I guess I should say *mansion*."

"Thanks," Brian said coolly.

A crystal chandelier the size of a piano was

hanging from the ceiling, and the walls had elaborate gold decorations on them. *Just this hallway is practically the size of my house,* Aaron thought.

Brian had invited Aaron to come over to his house after school to go over the list of people already in the club and to talk about possible new members.

"Do you have any brothers and sisters?" Aaron asked, as he followed Brian into a living room that looked like something out of a museum. The ceilings were higher than any Aaron had ever seen and the furniture looked as if it were all about three hundred years old. There was a deep red carpet on the floor and big paintings of different old men hanging on the walls.

"No, just me," Brian said.

"I was expecting you to say that you have eight brothers and sisters," Aaron joked. "I mean, your house is so big and everything."

Brian smirked as he sat down on the enormous white couch in the center of the room. "You think this is big?" he asked.

Aaron looked around the room. It was about the size of the basketball court at school. "Yeah, I think it's huge," he said as he sat down in an uncomfortable antique chair next to the couch.

"Well, this is teensy compared to my old house," Brian said. He stretched out his legs and put his sneakers up on the couch.

"It is?" Aaron asked incredulously.

"Sure," Brian said. "Our last place, in Beverly Hills, was about five times the size of this one."

Aaron couldn't even imagine a house that big. He'd never thought of his old house as small, but compared with Brian's, it was about the size of an anthill.

"Do you want something to eat and drink?" Brian asked as he lifted up a bell from the coffee table and rang it.

"That would be great," Aaron said.

Seconds later, an older man wearing what looked like a tuxedo walked into the room.

"Yes, sir?" the man said to Brian in an English accent.

"Hey, Harvey, bring us something to munch on," Brian commanded.

"Certainly, sir," Harvey replied, then he walked back out of the room.

Wow . . . a servant . . . just like in the movies, Aaron thought.

"OK, let's get to work," Brian said. "Let me see your list of people who are already in the group."

Aaron quickly handed him the piece of paper from his notebook. "At the bottom of the page, I've written down the names of some people who I think are really great," he said proudly. "You know, some people who I think would be good for the club."

The two boys sat in silence while Brian studied the list. He took a red pencil out of his shirt pocket and made little comments next to some of the names.

"Here you are, sirs," Harvey said as walked back into the room carrying a large silver platter.

Aaron gasped. On the tray were six small chocolate cakes, four sandwiches, a basket of tortilla chips, little bowls of guacamole and salsa, and four different kinds of sodas.

"If this is an afternoon snack, I'd like to know what kind of stuff you guys have for dinner around here," Aaron said, chuckling.

Brian grunted and stuck his hand into the basket of chips, keeping his eyes glued to the list. Harvey turned around and left the room as quickly as he'd entered it.

Aaron hungrily eyed the food in front of him, waiting for Brian to grab a sandwich or something.

"Aren't you going to have anything?" Brian finally asked after a few minutes had gone by.

"I didn't want to eat if you're not going to," Aaron said politely.

"Oh, please, go ahead," Brian said. "It'll all end up in the garbage anyway, so you might as well go for it."

Carefully, Aaron picked up one of the delicate, small white plates with little red rosebuds. He took half a sandwich, a cake, and a handful of chips. "This is my idea of heaven," he said eagerly. "At my house, an afternoon snack is an apple and a glass of milk."

"What a drag," Brian mumbled, still looking at the list.

"Yeah, it is," Aaron said, although it had never really bothered him in the past.

"I see that you put Randy Mason on the list," Brian said.

"He's a great guy," Aaron said enthusiastically. "He's really smart and funny."

"Uh-huh," Brian said, obviously unimpressed.

"When I was home sick for a week earlier this year, Randy came over to my house every day to give me my homework assignments," Aaron continued, his voice becoming a little urgent.

"How sweet," Brian said sarcastically.

Aaron smothered a gasp as Brian scratched a line right through Randy's name.

"He's just not *IN* material," Brian said, dipping a chip into the guacamole.

Aaron felt his heart drop. *I guess I don't have as much influence over Brian as I thought.*

Aaron helped himself to some more food as Brian continued to study the list. "Janet Howell's really rich, isn't she?" Brian asked.

"Yeah, she is," Aaron responded, though he didn't see what that had to do with anything. "She lives in a big mansion next door to her cousin, Lila Fowler."

"Janet's definitely in," Brian said, putting a check by her name. "In fact, she's exactly the kind of person we're looking for."

"Yeah," Aaron said, even though he really didn't get what Brian was talking about. Even the Unicorn Club, the snobbiest club he knew of, had some members who didn't have a lot of money.

Brian looked back down at the list. "Isn't Amy Sutton that ugly girl in Hairnet's class?" Brian asked.

"I wouldn't call her *ugly*," Aaron said. "She's not exactly a beauty or anything, but she's really nice and smart."

"I thought she was in Brooke's club already," Brian said.

"Well, she is, but I thought we could ask her to join our club," Aaron said. "She could be a really good asset."

"Look, we have a reputation to build. We have to keep our standards high. You do agree, don't you?" Brian looked at him fixedly.

"Oh, absolutely," Aaron said. "One hundred percent."

Seven

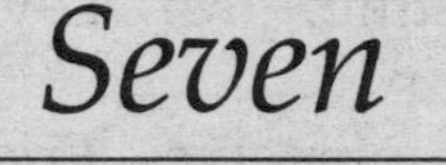

"He is just *too* cute to be a teacher, if you ask me." Jessica sighed dreamily as Mr. Levin walked into the social studies classroom on Thursday morning.

Elizabeth laughed. "This is a record, Jess. You've been awake in social studies class for four days straight. Maybe if you had handsome teachers in all your classes, you'd get better grades."

"Very funny," Jessica responded.

"Please be quiet, everyone," Mrs. Arnette said. "Mr. Levin is back with us again today, so please give him your full attention."

"He's already got mine," Jessica whispered.

"Good morning, folks," Mr. Levin said. "I'm here today to see how the two clubs are coming along. Brooke, why don't you tell me about your club."

Brooke stood up and smiled. "Well, the theme of our club is the environment," she said proudly.

Elizabeth heard someone snickering behind her. She turned around and saw Brian laughing and whispering something to Aaron.

"That's interesting," Mr. Levin said. "Tell me more."

"We're calling ourselves *Friends of the Land,"* Brooke said.

"Give me a break," Brian whispered loudly enough for Elizabeth to hear.

"And what kinds of things will your group be doing?" Mr. Levin asked. If he heard Brian's rude comment, he didn't acknowledge it.

"We're going to meet twice a week to clean up different areas around town," Brooke explained. "This afternoon we're all going to pick up cans and trash around the parking lot at Casey's."

"How wonderful!" Mrs. Arnette exclaimed, clapping her hands together.

"How juvenile," Brian mumbled.

"Brian, why don't you give us an update on your group," Mr. Levin said.

Elizabeth watched as Brian stood up next to his desk. He ran a hand through his dark hair and looked around the room as if he owned it.

"It's cool," Brian said. "So far I haven't laid down too many rules—mostly I'm working on membership right now."

"Membership?" Mr. Levin asked. "Didn't you

already choose who will be in your group?"

"Yeah, well, I've decided to expand the club to include people not in this class. That's OK, right? I mean, you said I could do whatever I want."

"Absolutely," Mr. Levin confirmed. "Does this mean that anyone one who wants to join your club can?"

Brian laughed. "No way. Actually, I might have to cut some of the original members to make room for some of the new people."

Concerned murmurs floated around the room, and Elizabeth saw a couple of people looking really upset.

"What are you basing your membership on?" Mr. Levin asked.

"That's kind of hard to say," Brian replied. "I'm going by more of a gut feeling."

Gut feeling? What's that supposed to mean? Elizabeth wondered.

"Hmm." Mr. Levin seemed to be carefully considering what Brian had said. "And what kind of things will your group be doing?"

"Mainly, just hanging out together," Brian said. "It's a social kind of thing. Of course, there will be a bunch of rules to follow. Like, for example, everyone's wearing black T-shirts and black armbands."

Mr. Levin looked around the room. "I see they are. And what are you going to do if people don't follow the rules and, say, violate the dress code?"

"So far that hasn't been a problem," Brian said

proudly. "I mean, who wouldn't want to show that they were a part of my group?"

"That's for sure," Lila murmured. She was sitting on the other side of Jessica and wearing a tight ribbed black T-shirt.

"But if anyone *does* find out that a club member isn't following the rules"—Brian looked around the classroom slowly and seriously—"that person should report the violation to me, and I'll take it from there."

Jessica shot Elizabeth a warning look, which Elizabeth pretended to ignore. Brian was seeming creepier and creepier to her—he sounded almost sinister.

She looked at Mr. Levin. Instead of looking angry or alarmed, he was smiling at Brian pleasantly. "Do you have organized meetings?" he asked.

"Yeah, we do," Brian said. "And there's one this afternoon at Casey's."

"Awesome," Melissa McCormick gushed.

"I can't wait," Jessica said.

"There's going to be a list posted on my locker at the end of the day," Brian said. "If a name's on the list, then that person's invited to the meeting."

"And if it's not?" Mr. Levin asked.

"Then they're out of the running," Brian answered.

The room grew completely silent, and Elizabeth saw true fear creep across many faces. *How can this one person have so much power over all these people?* Elizabeth wondered.

"I'm sure I'll be on that list," Jessica said to Elizabeth. "And you better start acting enthusiastic if you want to be on it."

Elizabeth sighed and began doodling on her notebook. *How can Jessica take such stupid rules so seriously?* she wondered. *Why is everyone getting so swept up in this club stuff?*

Jessica practically ran out of her last class on Thursday when the bell rang. She couldn't wait another minute to see if her name was on Brian's list.

Of course I'll make the list, she assured herself. *I mean, I'm one of the most popular girls in school.* Still, as she went down the hall her heart was thumping hard from anxiety. She couldn't relax until she knew for sure that Brian had chosen her.

A big group of people were gathered around Brian's locker, fighting to get a look at the list. Jessica spotted Lila in the sea of people.

"Do you see my name, Lila?" she called out.

"Yeah, you're on it," Lila shouted over the heads of the frenzied crowd.

"How about me?" Janet asked as she raced up behind Jessica.

"You're on it, too," Lila answered.

"All right!" Janet exclaimed, giving Jessica a high-five. "We made the cut."

Jessica smiled to herself. Obviously, Janet wasn't

quite as sure that she'd be chosen as she'd pretended.

"Hey, check it out," Lila said, pointing to Winston Egbert, who was fighting his way through the crowd to check for his name. "Can you believe Winston actually thinks he stands a chance?"

Jessica giggled. "Poor guy," she said, shaking her head. "Some people just don't have a clue."

"I think cluelessness is contagious," Janet said, pointing at Maria Slater, who studied the list and then turned around and walked away down the hall. "That girl really ought to know that she's just *not* a candidate for an exciting, exclusive club like Brian's," Janet continued authoritatively. "She's way too boring."

"Speaking of boring," Lila said to Jessica, with a toss of her hair, "I was sort of surprised to see your sister on the list. She's not exactly the *IN* type."

Jessica felt her face grow warm. She had to admit, Elizabeth had been a little uptight about the club in the last couple of days, but Jessica didn't like it when other people criticized her sister. "Elizabeth is *not* boring," she said defensively. "She's the total *IN* type."

"Look, there's a reason Winston and Maria aren't on the list, and they *are* two of your sister's best friends," Janet pointed out.

"Elizabeth has a lot of different sides of her personality," Jessica argued. "And she has a lot of different kinds of friends."

"Yeah, well, whatever," Lila said, taking out a lip gloss from her backpack.

"You guys will have to see for yourselves," Jessica said huffily. "Elizabeth will be a great asset to *IN*."

"See you this afternoon, Aaron," Bruce Patman said as he passed by Aaron in the hallway. "Four o'clock at Casey's, right?"

"Uh, yeah, right," Aaron said.

Aaron smiled as he continued walking down the hall. Bruce and he weren't exactly great friends, but he felt good about the bond *IN* was already creating among its members, and he loved getting attention from popular seventh- and eighth-graders. He'd always been popular, but this was different. People were looking up to him as some kind of authority—it was almost as though Brian's influence was rubbing off on him a little.

"Great shirt, Aaron," Janet said as she walked by.

"Thanks," Aaron said, surprised. Since when had Janet Howell been interested in his clothes?

Well, I better get used to it, he decided, sighing with satisfaction. *I'm definitely a big deal on campus now that I'm tight with Brian.*

As he continued walking down the hall, his gait changed to a proud stride. He felt on top of the world. *Maybe Brian will make me the vice president of the club. Maybe—*

"Hey, Aaron, wait up!"

Aaron turned around to see Randy coming toward him at an urgent pace.

Aaron felt his heart sink as he remembered how he assured his friend he'd get his name on the list—and how Brian refused to let Randy in the club.

Randy slowed down as he got closer. "Hey, what happened?"

"What do you mean?" Aaron asked innocently, even though he knew perfectly well what Randy was talking about.

"I thought you were going to talk to Brian about getting me into the club," Randy said.

Aaron looked down at his sneakers and swallowed hard. "I'm sorry," he said in a whisper. "I *did* talk to him."

Randy frowned. "So what did he say? Did he say he didn't like me or something?"

"No, not at all," Aaron said quickly. "I thought he was going to ask you to join."

Aaron couldn't bring himself to tell Randy the truth—that apparently Brian really *didn't* seem to like his friend, and that Aaron's recommendation didn't matter to him.

Randy stared at him for a moment. "Well, he didn't," he said flatly.

"I'm sorry," Aaron said weakly.

Randy let out a defeated sigh. "I just don't understand it," he said, shaking his head. "I mean, I've really made an effort with him."

Aaron was trying not to look at his friend. "I just don't know what to say," he murmured.

"I even invited him to come to the synagogue with me on Monday night for a special dinner they were having for kids," Randy went on.

Aaron felt a wave of sympathy for his friend. Somehow, he didn't think that going to a synagogue dinner would be at all the kind of thing that Brian would be into, and he felt bad that Randy was trying so hard.

"I bet he would've really liked it, too, but he said he had other plans," Randy continued. "It's too bad, because they served steak and there were a lot of pretty girls and stuff."

"Sounds great," Aaron said, managing a small smile.

Randy sighed again. "I just thought that since he was new in town and everything, it would be a good way for him to get to know some people."

"That was really nice of you," Aaron said.

"Yeah, well, I guess Brian didn't think so," Randy said glumly.

"Randy, I wish I could do something to help, I really do. It's just that, well, Brian seems pretty stubborn," Aaron said. "Once he makes up his mind about something, he doesn't usually change it."

Randy shook his head. "It's not your fault."

Aaron couldn't help feeling that it was—that he should have tried harder to get Brian to change his mind. "I'm sorry anyway," he said.

"Well, whatever," Randy said, shrugging. "I guess there's not much point thinking about it anymore. Hey, how's your grandpa?"

"He's fine I guess," Aaron said, feeling guilty that Randy was being so nice when Aaron hadn't really stood up for him.

"Well, tell him I said hello," Randy said.

"Yeah, sure," Aaron said quickly, suddenly realizing he couldn't bear to be around Randy anymore—he was acting so considerate. "Well, I gotta go. I have stuff to do. See ya!"

Aaron booked down the hall, giving his friend a brief wave over his shoulder.

Eight

"Can we end a little early today?" Jessica asked as she completed a cartwheel at Booster practice on Thursday. The Boosters were the baton-twirling and cheering squad for Sweet Valley Middle School. The members were all Unicorns except for Amy Sutton and Winston Egbert, neither of whom could make practice today.

"We still have another routine to go over," Janet pointed out.

"I just thought we could use the extra time to freshen up before that meeting at Casey's this afternoon," Jessica said.

Janet folded her arms and considered for a moment. "I guess that's a good idea," she said. "I wouldn't even mind stopping by my house to get changed first."

Jessica felt a flutter of excitement—the *IN* spirit was building over the entire school. She loved being a part of something this important. "Yeah, maybe I'll put on a new outfit, too," she said eagerly.

"I heard a rumor that Brian was going to buy all of us ice cream at Casey's today," Tamara said as she went into a split. "Can you imagine how expensive that will be?"

"Well, it's no big deal for him," Janet said as she put away her pom-poms. "His family's loaded."

"Really?" Lila asked, looking intrigued. "How do you know?"

"My dad told me last night," Janet said. "Apparently, his father's a big movie producer."

Jessica's eyes lit up. "How cool! Maybe his father will put us in a movie!"

"Yeah, right, Jessica," Lila said wearily. "Dream on."

Jessica tossed her hair. "Well, I'm not writing off the possibility. An aspiring actress has to keep her eyes open for opportunities, you know." Jessica loved anything that had to do with the spotlight and wanted to be a movie star or a model when she grew up.

"Well, whether or not we get to be in a movie," Janet said, "the fact that Brian's father is a producer makes being in his club even more glamorous. We'll probably get to meet all kinds of movie stars and stuff if we hang around with him."

Ellen cleared her throat. "Do you think you guys

could talk about this when I'm not around?"

Jessica turned to look at Ellen. "I take it you weren't invited to the meeting today, huh?"

Ellen glared at her. "Gee, Jessica, how'd you guess?" she said sarcastically. Then she stormed over to the other side of the gym to gather up her things.

"Look, Ellen, if you come with the rest of us to the meeting, I'm sure Brian won't care," Mary said.

Ellen flung her backpack over her back. "Why would I want to go to a meeting where I'm not welcome?" she asked hotly.

"Maybe we could talk to him and get him to change his mind," Mary offered.

"Look, if he wanted me in the club, he would have invited me," Ellen said. "It's pretty clear that he just doesn't like me."

"I'm sure that's not true," Jessica protested, even though she realized that for some reason, it *had* to have been true.

Ellen ignored Jessica's protests and started toward the door. "I hope you guys have fun," she said. "Enjoy your free ice cream."

For a moment, everyone stood around the gym looking at one another in silence.

"It *is* kind of weird that Ellen wasn't invited," Mandy said finally. "I mean, every other Unicorn was."

Lila frowned. "Yeah, I don't get it."

"Well," Janet said briskly, tossing her backpack

over her shoulder, "I guess we should feel even more honored that *we* were invited. Obviously, just being a Unicorn wasn't the only reason we were all chosen."

Jessica felt another burst of excitement. The requirements for membership in Brian's club *were* a little mysterious, but she didn't care. The important thing was that *she* was a member of the hippest and most exclusive club in Sweet Valley!

"How's that article coming along?" Elizabeth asked Winston on Thursday afternoon in the *Sixers* office.

Winston sighed heavily. "OK, I guess."

Elizabeth put down her pen and looked at Winston. "You don't sound too thrilled about it. I thought you'd be happy to write about computers, since that's your specialty."

"Mmm," Winston mumbled.

"What's that?" Elizabeth pressed.

Winston pushed away his notebook. "Computers aren't exactly the problem," he said glumly.

Elizabeth furrowed her brow. "Then what's bothering you? You don't seem like yourself today."

Winston looked around the room, then leaned toward Elizabeth. "It's about Brian's club," he whispered.

"What about it?" Elizabeth whispered back.

"Well, the second meeting is this afternoon at

Casey's," Winston said, as if that explained everything.

"So? What does that have to do with you?" Elizabeth asked.

Winston took a deep breath. "Nothing. That's the point."

"I'm not following you," Elizabeth said.

"I wasn't invited to go," Winston said.

Elizabeth groaned inwardly. It was one thing for Jessica and all her silly friends to become caught up in this whole club business, but Winston wasn't normally such a crowd follower. Brian Boyd obviously had even more influence than she thought.

"And I've tried everything to be invited to join the group," Winston continued.

Elizabeth felt a strange twinge of worry. "What do you mean *everything*?"

Winston took a deep breath. "Well, on Monday he was sitting next to me when I got back my math test," he began to explain. "And he saw that I got an *A* on it. He started complimenting me and everything, saying that he'd had the feeling that I was really smart." Winston paused and looked at the table. "Well, we started talking. He seemed really friendly, and I thought, 'Excellent, the coolest guy in school likes me'. Then he asked if I could help him."

"Help him with his math?" Elizabeth asked, trying to sound neutral even though she had the feeling she wasn't going to like how this story would turn out.

"Yeah, help him in math," Winston confirmed. "Anyway, I told him I'd be happy to tutor him after school."

"That was nice of you," Elizabeth said.

"Yeah, that's what he said, too," Winston told her. He hesitated once more, clicking his pen. "Then he asked if I'd just give him the assignment, since he didn't have time to have a lesson on that particular day."

Elizabeth felt her breath catch. "And you agreed?"

Winston nodded cautiously. "I guess I just wanted him to like me," he answered. "He's so popular and everything, and he was being so friendly. I figured he just wanted to borrow my homework that one time, and then we could be friends."

Elizabeth folded her arms. "Let me guess—he asked to borrow it again."

"Yes," Winston admitted weakly.

"And you did it," Elizabeth said flatly.

Winston nodded and looked down at his notebook.

"And he still didn't put your name on the list today," Elizabeth said, feeling her heart beat faster with rage.

"Nope," he said.

"Well, consider yourself lucky," Elizabeth said. She stood up and stormed out of the office. *I smell a rat and his name is Brian Boyd,* she thought as she stomped down the hall.

"Hey, Lizzie!" Jessica called as she ran out of the gymnasium and saw Elizabeth walking quickly in her direction. "Ready for—"

"I'm ready to talk to you," Elizabeth interrupted in a huff.

Jessica studied her sister's face. It was bright red. "We should stop in the bathroom before the meeting," Jessica told her. "You definitely need to splash your face."

"I'm not going to any meeting and neither should you," Elizabeth informed her.

"What are you talking about? Of course we're—"

"Sit down," Elizabeth broke in, as she pulled Jessica down on a bench.

"Please tell me what this is about," Jessica said. "We have to get to that meeting and I have to freshen up first."

"I really think that Brian person is bad news," Elizabeth said.

Jessica sighed impatiently. *Why is she doing this now, when I'm in a hurry?* she thought. "We've been over this a hundred times. I like Brian and so does everyone else except you."

"I just have a really strong feeling about this," Elizabeth said. "I don't think you should have anything to do with Brian or that stupid club."

"Listen, Lizzie, I know you try to do everything

you can to avoid anything that's really cool, but just this once—"

"I just talked to Winston, and he's really upset about not being invited to that meeting," Elizabeth broke in abruptly.

"Give me a break," Jessica said, about to lose her patience.

"Winston's a great person," Elizabeth said firmly.

Jessica rolled her eyes. "I know he's your friend and everything, but even you have to admit he's not exactly *IN* material."

"I don't know what *IN* material is," Elizabeth said. "And I'm not sure anyone else does for that matter—except Brian."

Jessica sighed heavily. "So Winston isn't invited to the meeting," she said. "Is that why you're acting like a total nutcase?"

"It's not just that," Elizabeth replied. "Brian did something to Winston that wasn't nice. He asked—"

"I don't even want to hear it, Elizabeth," Jessica said, holding her hand up. "I'm sorry Brian wasn't nice to Winston, but there are two sides to every story."

"Well, I have every reason to believe Winston's side," Elizabeth said.

Jessica glanced at her watch. "Look, I'll make a deal with you," she said. "You come to the meeting with me now, and then we'll have another conversation about this."

"And what good will that do?" Elizabeth asked.

"You'll be able to see for yourself if Brian's really as bad as you think he is," Jessica said.

"Forget it," Elizabeth said. "I already know he is. I went to that first meeting, remember?"

Jessica gritted her teeth. She thought about what Brian had said about ratting on people who disobeyed his rules. She didn't see how she could rat on her own sister—she had to do *something* to make Elizabeth shape up.

She put on her sweetest, most desperate face—the one that usually got Elizabeth to do what she wanted. "Can't you please just do this for me?" she pleaded. "I'll return the favor. I promise."

"No," Elizabeth said firmly.

"Please," Jessica said even more urgently.

"No," Elizabeth repeated.

"I'll do all your chores for a week," Jessica offered hopefully.

"I don't care if you do them for a year," Elizabeth said. "I'm not going to that meeting and that's final."

Jessica stood up from the bench. "I'll never forget how you let me down today."

Elizabeth stood up, too, and looked Jessica directly in the eye. "And I'll never forget how you didn't listen to my advice. I really think this guy is trouble."

"And I'm just as sure that he's not," Jessica snapped.

Why do I have to have the most stubborn identical twin sister in all history? Jessica thought, as she hurried away.

"Hey, listen up, everyone," Brian commanded from the booth where he was sitting at Casey's on Thursday afternoon. "The meeting has officially started."

Aaron, sitting right next to Brian, felt a thrill pass through his body. It seemed a little silly, but he almost felt as if he were sitting next to a king or the president.

"OK, first item of business," Brian began. "I want everyone to take a piece of paper, like a napkin or something, when they leave here."

"What for?" Rick Hunter asked.

"To throw on the ground around the parking lot," Brian said with a satisfied smile. "Brooke's little club is going to be here in a while to clean it up. We might as well give them something to do."

"That's fantastic," Bruce said. "Hey, you're all right, man."

Aaron squirmed in his seat. He couldn't quite see the point of throwing garbage around. Then again, he'd always liked pulling pranks on Halloween and stuff—maybe this was sort of the same thing.

"Second item on the agenda," Brian continued. "I want you guys to all come to a party I'm having at my house on Saturday night."

People responded with cheers and applause.

Aaron smiled, but he had a funny feeling in his stomach. Brian hadn't mentioned anything about a party to him. It wasn't that big a deal, but Brian *had* been confiding everything to him lately about the club. *Well, maybe he just decided a little while ago and didn't have a chance to tell me,* he reasoned.

"Now, it's obviously a really exclusive party, so don't say anything to anyone about it," Brian went on. "Only the people at this meeting are invited."

Jessica's eyes widened. "What kind of party is it going to be?"

Brian smiled broadly. "Let's just say it's going to be the party of the century. A band's coming in from L.A., and it's going to be catered by La Maison Jacques.

"Sounds amazing," Lila said breathlessly.

Bruce folded his arms and smiled.

The party sounds like it's going to cost a fortune, Aaron thought. La Maison Jacques was the fanciest, most expensive restaurant in Sweet Valley. Aaron had gone there a couple of times with his family on special occasions.

"Can I help you set up for the party?" Melissa McCormick asked, leaning forward eagerly.

"Me, too!" Tamara Chase added.

"Perfect," Brian said. "Melissa and Tamara are on setup duty. Who wants to be in charge of cleanup?"

Aaron felt a tiny jolt. Why would Brian want his guests to do cleanup? And who would volunteer to clean up after somebody's party before the party even happened?

"I'll do it!" Kimberly Haver announced.

Aaron glanced at Kimberly. She looked absolutely thrilled to be helping Brian out. As thrilled as Aaron himself had been when Brian made him his Special Assistant.

"Hey, you didn't bring anything to throw," Brian said to Aaron in Casey's parking lot at the end of the meeting. The club members were already starting to throw soda cans and napkins all around the parking lot, just as Brian had instructed.

"Oh, right, I forgot," Aaron said.

Brian handed Aaron a roll of toilet paper. "Here, take this. I stole it from the mens' room." He began laughing.

Aaron managed a laugh, too, even though he felt a little uncomfortable.

"So go ahead," Brian said, pushing him toward the crowd.

Reluctantly, Aaron walked through the parking lot, strewing toilet paper around on the ground.

"This is cool," Bruce said as he threw a big stack of paper napkins up in the air and watched them land all over the place.

I should lighten up, Aaron told himself, watching Bruce. *Everyone's having a good time. It's just a fun prank.*

"Hey, who's old wreck is that?" Brian asked

Aaron. He was pointing to a beat-up old car that had scratched paint.

Before Aaron could answer, Melissa McCormick waved to her mother, who was driving the car, and hopped inside.

"That's Melissa's parents' car?" Brian asked incredulously.

Aaron shrugged. "Yeah, I guess so."

"What does her father do for a living?" Brian asked.

Aaron stared blankly at Brian. *Why does he want to know that?* he wondered. Aaron barely knew what anyone's parents at Sweet Valley did. It just wasn't something he thought about.

Before Aaron could answer, Casey came running out to the parking lot. "What's going on out here?" he demanded. His face was bright red, and sweat was running down his forehead.

Aaron froze and looked desperately at Brian.

Brian wore a concerned expression. "We were just cleaning up," he told Casey as he reached down to pick up some scraps of paper. "I'm afraid a bunch of kids—Brooke Dennis and some others—were here throwing all this junk around. I guess this sort of thing is some people's idea of a prank."

Casey was breathing hard. "But it looked like—I thought you—"

Brian patted him on the arm and looked kindly into his eyes. "When I saw what they were doing, I got this group of people together and asked them to help me clean up."

Casey looked around. The members of *IN* had started to pick up the garbage they had thrown around. *It's like Brian's voice has some special power,* Aaron thought.

Casey gave Brian a hug. "Thank you, son," he said. "You're a good boy."

"My pleasure," Brian said. "You go back inside and we'll finish cleaning up this mess."

As soon as Casey was gone, Brian snapped his fingers. "Drop all your trash, and let's take off!" he commanded.

Aaron began walking away just as Brooke and her club approached, carrying big green trash bags.

"Good grief, this is a disaster area!" Brooke shrieked. "I've never seen it look so disgusting."

Brian shook his head sympathetically. "Yeah, it looks like you really have your work cut out for you," he said. "It's a good thing you're here to clean up the environment." He slapped Aaron on the back. "Come on, Aaron, let's go."

Aaron looked around at the horrible scene. "Maybe we should stay and help Brooke," he said softly.

Brian laughed. "You're kidding, right?"

Aaron felt a knot in his stomach. "Oh, of course, I'm kidding," he lied.

* * *

"Jessica! Wait up!" Brian yelled.

Jessica turned around and beamed, hoping that her hair wasn't getting mussed up. She had made it out of Casey's parking lot and had run halfway down the block.

"Hey, Brian, how's it going?" Jessica asked, trying to catch her breath.

"How'd you like the second meeting?" Brian asked.

"It was great," Jessica said, flipping her hair out of her face. "Those pranks are so much fun." The truth was that she didn't really understand the point of throwing trash all over the place, and she wanted to have as little to do with garbage as possible. But if Brian thought it was cool, she wasn't about to question him. He was so totally charming and adorable.

"I couldn't help noticing that your sister missed the second meeting," Brian said.

"Oh, I know," Jessica said, thinking fast. "She had a big article she had to finish for the *Sixers*. She's really sorry, and she still wants to be a member of the club."

Brian frowned. "Missing the second meeting— I'd say that's a pretty big violation of the rules of the club, wouldn't you? I have to wonder if Elizabeth is really *IN* material."

"Oh, believe me, she's *IN* material all right," Jessica insisted. "Elizabeth thinks the club's the greatest, and she'd be devastated if she couldn't be in it."

"I'm beginning to wonder," Brian said, folding his arms. "She's been really unenthusiastic. I'm surprised you don't have more influence on her. She *is* your twin sister, after all."

He looked at her with a sparkle of challenge in his eyes—a sparkle that excited her and frightened her at the same time. A sparkle that somehow told her she *had* to keep Elizabeth from breaking any more rules.

"I *do* have influence over her," Jessica said in a rush. "But it's just that she's been really busy lately. Could you just give her one more chance?"

Brian sighed deeply. "I guess so," he said. "Tell her she's invited to my party on Saturday night."

"That's great," Jessica said, smiling with relief. "She'll be thrilled."

"Make sure she understands how exclusive the party is," Brian said. "I mean, she should realize what a privilege it is for her to even be invited."

"Oh, I'll definitely make sure," Jessica said.

Nine

"I need to talk to you," Jessica said as she stormed into Elizabeth's room on Thursday night.

Elizabeth was sitting on her bed, reading. She looked up slowly and held her place in the book with her finger.

"Jessica, I'm in the middle of reading a great book," Elizabeth protested. "Can't we talk about whatever it is you want to talk about another time?"

Jessica plopped down next to Elizabeth on the bed. "What I have to talk to you about is more important than whatever book you're reading."

"Nothing could be more important than this book," Elizabeth said somberly.

Jessica grabbed the book from Elizabeth's hands and turned it over to look at the cover. *"The Diary of Anne Frank,"* she read out loud. "Who's Anne Frank?"

"She was a Jewish girl who had to hide from the Nazis with her family during World War Two," Elizabeth explained. "She lived in Amsterdam."

"She looks about our age," Jessica said, examining the picture of Anne Frank on the cover.

"She was just twelve when she and her family starting hiding in the attic of the house where her father worked," Elizabeth said quietly. "They hid there for two whole years."

"Two whole years in an attic!" Jessica exclaimed. "And they had to hide there because they were Jewish?"

Elizabeth nodded. "The Nazis were supposed to hunt down and kill Jews and homosexuals and gypsies and anyone else Adolf Hitler didn't like."

Jessica sat in silence for a moment, biting her lip. "What kind of stuff does Anne write about?" she asked finally.

"She writes about how every day her family lives in fear that they'll be found," Elizabeth answered softly.

"And were they ever found?" Jessica asked.

Elizabeth felt a lump in her throat. "That's the saddest part of all. The Nazis found her and her family and sent them to a concentration camp. Anne died there two months before the war ended."

Jessica spent another long moment staring at the picture of Anne Frank. "That's a horrible story," she said, her voice catching a little. "It's too sad to even think about."

"Yeah, it is," Elizabeth agreed. She cleared her throat. "Well, what did you want to talk to me about?"

"Oh, nothing," Jessica said abruptly. "It can wait until tomorrow."

"Hey, Anna, I'll see you tomorrow night, right?"

Elizabeth recognized Brian's voice from around the locker bank. It was Friday before homework, and she was at her locker, getting her books for her morning classes. She watched as Anna Reynolds walked by.

"What's with that Anna Reynolds girl?" Brian asked somebody Elizabeth couldn't see.

"What do you mean?" Ken Matthews asked.

"I just asked her a question, and she totally ignored me," Brian said.

"Oh, that's because she's hearing-impaired," Ken Matthews explained.

"You mean, deaf?" Brian asked loudly.

"Well, yeah, but I think now people call it hearing-impaired," Ken replied. "She understands sign language and she also reads lips."

"Sheesh, you'd never know it just from looking at her," Brian said. "I mean, she looks so normal and pretty and everything."

"Yeah, well, you'd be surprised at how well she gets along," Ken said. "It's like the only thing she can't do is hear."

"Uh-huh," Brian said dismissively.

"Next time, you should stand right in front of her so she can see you speaking," Ken told him.

"Yeah, I'm sure I'll really do that," Brian said, laughing.

Elizabeth closed her locker with a shudder. *There's no doubt about it—Brian Boyd is a major jerk,* she thought.

"OK, here's the list of people who are invited to the party," Brian said to Aaron in homeroom on Friday morning.

Aaron took the list from Brian. "It looks like some of the people who were at Casey's yesterday aren't listed."

"I had to make some changes," Brian explained. "Oh, and I need to ask you a favor."

"Sure, anything," Aaron said, starting to feel a little dismayed.

Brian handed Aaron another piece of paper. "These are the people who were invited but now need to be uninvited."

Aaron looked at some of the names. "And what do you want me to do?" he asked cautiously, afraid he already knew the answer.

"I want you to uninvite them," Brian said matter-of-factly.

Suddenly, Aaron had an unpleasant taste in his mouth. He looked at the "uninvited" list in distress. "But Melissa even volunteered to help you set up for the party," he pointed out. "Why isn't she invited anymore?"

Brian rolled his eyes. "Look, she's just not right

for *IN*," he said. "If we don't set some kind of standard, we might as well let the club be open to the whole school."

It just doesn't make sense, Aaron thought. *Melissa is one of the nicest people I know.*

"And what about Anna Reynolds?" Aaron asked. "She's never done anything bad to anyone in her life."

"That's not the point," Brian said.

So what is the point? Aaron wondered. Was Brian just being mean to people for the fun of it? But somehow he couldn't bring himself to ask. There was something about Brian's tone that was so certain, so forceful—as if he wouldn't put up with anyone crossing him.

"Oh, what are you doing after school today?" Brian asked, smiling openly at Aaron. "I was wondering if you'd like to go to the mall with me. I want to get some good CDs to dance to at the party."

Hearing the change in Brian's voice, Aaron couldn't help feeling a little flattered. Even if Brian wasn't always the nicest guy to people he didn't like, he was definitely nice to his friends—and Aaron was obviously one of his friends. He was glad Brian thought he was cool enough to hang out with.

Aaron smiled. "That'd be awesome," he told Brian.

"I still can't believe you guys cleaned up that entire parking lot," Elizabeth said to Amy and Maria at lunch on Friday.

"I can't either," Amy groaned.

"You can't imagine how disgusting it was," Maria said, scrunching up her face. "There was paper everywhere you looked."

"It's funny, but I never noticed Casey's parking lot was all that messy before," Elizabeth said.

"Me neither," Amy said. "I'm surprised the health inspectors don't give Casey a warning or something."

"I have to say, I think you're pretty lucky you're in Brian's club instead of ours, Elizabeth," Maria said. "We're an organized group of garbage collectors."

"*And* you get to go to Brian's super-exclusive party on Saturday—open only to members of *IN*," Amy said. "Everyone's talking about it, even though it's supposed to be a secret."

"Hey, guys, can I sit with you?" Melissa asked, approaching with her tray.

Elizabeth looked up and saw that Melissa's eyes were all puffy and red. "Of course," Elizabeth said. "Are you OK?"

Melissa sat down and wiped a tear away from her eye. "No, not really."

Amy frowned with concern. "Tell us what happened."

"It's about Brian's party," Melissa said, sniffling softly.

Her heart beating with dread, Elizabeth gently touched Melissa's arm. "What about it?" she asked.

Melissa took a deep breath. "Well, I was invited—at first."

Amy and Elizabeth exchanged glances. "What do you mean *at first*?" Amy asked.

"Well, I was really excited about it. I was even planning to help Brian set up and everything. But now Aaron just told me that I was uninvited," Melissa blurted out as tears started to well up.

"I can't believe that!" Elizabeth said.

Melissa just nodded listlessly.

Outraged, Elizabeth glanced around the cafeteria for Brian and Aaron, and her eyes fell on Anna. "Anna's sitting by herself, and she looks like she's been crying, too."

Elizabeth waved Anna over to the table. *I have a bad feeling this isn't just a coincidence,* she thought.

Anna walked slowly toward their table with her head hanging low. "Hi, guys," she said.

"What's wrong, Anna?" Maria asked.

"I don't really want to talk about it," Anna replied softly.

Elizabeth looked at Amy and then at Anna. "Are you upset about something having to do with Brian and his club?" she asked.

Anna nodded slowly.

"Were you uninvited from the party, too?" Melissa asked her.

Anna heaved a sigh and sat down at the table. "I just don't understand," she said. "Aaron didn't even give me any reason."

Elizabeth shook her head in disgust. "This is terrible. I can't believe that those guys would do anything this low—I didn't think even Brian Boyd was this big a jerk."

"I just wish I knew why Brian doesn't like me," Melissa said. "Maybe he doesn't think I'm cool enough or something."

"Please don't feel bad just because Brian Boyd doesn't want you in his stupid club," Elizabeth urged. "He's obviously deciding everything in a totally random way."

"I think you're right," Amy agreed. "It's almost impossible to figure out what he's basing membership on."

Anna sighed. "I still really wanted to go to that party."

"Listen, you guys, I have a great idea," Elizabeth announced. "We're going to have our own party at my house tomorrow night."

"But you're probably invited to Brian's party," Amy pointed out.

Elizabeth rolled her eyes. "Believe me, I'd rather hang out with you guys than go to some party of Brian Boyd's any day."

Ten

"Hey, check it out—the Flying Lizards have a new CD," Brian said to Aaron on Friday afternoon. He was holding up a CD at the record store in Sweet Valley Mall. "They're the coolest, aren't they?"

"Oh, yeah. They're awesome," Aaron said, even though he'd never heard of the Flying Lizards in his life. What was going on with him? What was it about Brian that made him feel he had to lie?

"Now, *this* is a hot new group," Brian said authoritatively, as he held up another CD. "I saw them in concert last month."

Aaron peered over at the CD. *The Jumping Jack-o'-Lanterns,* he read to himself. Another group he'd never heard of. He was beginning to feel completely out of it. He hoped that Brian wouldn't start asking him questions about the kind of music he listened to—he might think it was completely uncool.

"Oh, hey, speaking of concerts, were you able to score tickets for a Lakers game, like you promised?" Brian asked.

Aaron felt his chest tighten. He had been hoping Brian had forgotten all about the Lakers tickets. He almost would have preferred for Brian to ask him about his favorite Jumping Jack-o'-Lanterns songs. Looking down at the row of CDs, he flipped through them urgently as if he were looking for something specific. "Oh . . . yeah . . . well, I'm still working on it," he said without looking at Brian.

"Cool," Brian said. "They're playing the Bulls next week, and I really want to go to that game."

"Me, too," Aaron said, moving quickly to another section of the store. He didn't want to talk anymore about Lakers tickets. *Maybe Grandpa could lend me some money,* he thought. *Mom and Dad probably wouldn't like that, but I could ask Grandpa if we could keep it a secret.*

After about ten minutes of browsing around on his own, Aaron was ready to go home. He'd been getting behind on his homework lately. *Besides, I should be spending more time with Grandpa,* he thought.

When he started back toward the front of the store, he stopped in his tracks. Brian was in the middle of the store putting a CD in his backpack!

Aaron felt his whole body shaking. He'd never

seen anyone steal anything—and Brian had enough money to buy every CD in the store. "I'll meet you out front," he said weakly to Brian.

"I'm coming, too," Brian said.

To Aaron's horror, Brian followed closely behind him on the way out of the store.

"Walk fast," Brian instructed as they walked through the mall.

Aaron's heart was racing, and he felt the sweat running down his forehead. He was too afraid to turn around to see if they were being followed.

When they got outside, Brian looked at Aaron's face and started laughing hysterically.

"What's so funny?" Aaron asked feebly, feeling his shoulders tighten.

"You are," Brian said, pointing at Aaron. "You look like you just saw a ghost."

Aaron didn't know what to do. *Should I tell Brian I saw what he did?* he wondered. *Should I tell him to go return the CD?*

Before Aaron said anything, Brian opened up his backpack and held it up to Aaron for him to look inside. "Not bad," Brian said proudly. "Now we can really party down!"

Aaron fought back the tears he felt creeping up on him. Inside Brian's bag were at least ten brand-new CDs—all stolen.

"Pretty awesome, huh?" Brian said with a laugh. "Bet you didn't know I was so talented."

Aaron glanced at Brian and saw a strange glint

in his eyes—friendly but at the same time a little threatening. Aaron swallowed hard. "That's really cool," he said softly. "Way to go."

"You make the greatest french toast, Dad," Elizabeth said on Saturday morning at the breakfast table.

"Actually, I can't take the credit for this," Mr. Wakefield said. "You have your sister to thank."

Elizabeth raised an eyebrow at Jessica. "*You* made it?" she asked incredulously.

"Yep," Jessica said proudly. "I know it's your favorite, so I got up early to make it."

Steven looked up from his plate. "You got up early to cook? What's the occasion? Are they having a big sale at the mall or something?"

"Very funny," Jessica said. "I just wanted to do something nice for Elizabeth."

Elizabeth set her fork down. "OK, get it over with. What is it this time?"

"What do you mean?" Jessica asked innocently.

"You know perfectly well what I mean," Elizabeth said. "Why'd you get up early to make french toast for me?"

"Sheesh, can't I just do something special for you without having a reason?" Jessica asked.

Elizabeth looked at Jessica impatiently. "Oh, be real."

Jessica giggled. "Well, OK, OK. There is one little thing I want you to do," she admitted.

"I knew it," Elizabeth said triumphantly.

"I can't wait to hear this," Steven said, smirking.

"It's about tonight," Jessica said sweetly.

"What about it?" Elizabeth asked.

Jessica took a deep breath. "You have to do something for me, and I know what your reaction is going to be—"

"If this is about Brian's party," Elizabeth interrupted, "I don't want to hear it."

"Isn't Brian that new student in school who's the leader of that club?" Mrs. Wakefield asked.

"That's the one," Elizabeth said, making a face as if she smelled something rotten.

"Geez, Elizabeth, why do you have to make such awful faces everytime we talk about Brian," Jessica said with a shudder. "You haven't even really gotten to know him."

"We've had this exact conversation about one hundred times already," Elizabeth said, pouring syrup on her french toast. "I don't like Brian Boyd, I don't want to like Brian Boyd, and there's no way you can convince me to like Brian Boyd."

"I'm not understanding this conversation," Mr. Wakefield said.

"That makes two of us," Mrs. Wakefield said. "Could someone explain the problem?"

"Brian's having this great party, and he wants Elizabeth to go to it," Jessica said.

"So what does that have to do with you?" Steven asked.

Jessica glared at Steven. "Could you please stay out of this?"

"I'm wondering the same thing, honey," Mrs. Wakefield said. "Why is it so important to you that Elizabeth goes to the party?"

Jessica felt like her whole family was ganging up on her. "Because . . . well, just because it is," she said. She knew why it was important, but it was too complicated to explain.

"Oh, that's a really good reason," Steven said.

"Look, Brian will be mad at me if Elizabeth doesn't go to the party," Jessica said. "He might not even let me be a member of the club anymore."

Mr. Wakefield frowned. "If that's the kind of person he is, maybe you don't want to be in his club."

"That's not even the worst of it," Elizabeth said. "Believe me, that guy is bad news."

Jessica groaned and got up from the table. *This is useless,* she decided. *I'll just have to wait and talk to her when we're alone.*

"Hey, Wakefield, I expect to see you tonight."

Elizabeth was riding her bike to Amy's house on Saturday, taking the long route through one of Sweet Valley's wealthiest neighborhoods. She glanced to her left and saw Brian standing at the edge of an expansive front yard, his arms folded, an arrogant grin on his face. Aaron was standing right next to him.

Elizabeth brought her bike to a stop. She didn't especially feel like chatting with Brian Boyd, but she didn't want him to get the idea he could tell her what to do or where to go. "See me where?" she asked.

"At my party," Brian said. "Your sister was supposed to invite you."

"Oh, yeah, she told me about it," Elizabeth said coolly.

"So are you coming?" Brian asked.

"No, I'm not," she said, then started to bike away.

Brian walked quickly after her and grabbed her by the arm.

"Get off of me," Elizabeth said, shaking her arm out of his grasp. "What do you want?"

"I want to know what your problem is," Brian said, his eyes narrowing.

Elizabeth glanced back at Aaron, but he was just staring at the ground, not saying a word.

She met Brian's eyes. "I don't have a problem," she snapped.

"Every person in this school is dying to be in my club except you," Brian said. "You've been given a bunch of opportunities to join, and you haven't made the slightest bit of effort. It's an assignment, and you're totally ignoring it."

His use of the word *assignment* made her shiver—it was as though he thought he was a king or something. And she realized just then that she really didn't care that obeying Brian Boyd's orders *was* an assignment. Something told her that it was a dangerous one—one she shouldn't follow. "Did it ever occur to you that I'm just not impressed by you or your stupid club?" she said, her heart beating hard.

"You're going to be sorry you ever said that," Brian said through clenched teeth.

The expression on his face was so evil, it made Elizabeth's skin crawl. "Your threats don't scare me," she informed him, then she broke away, pedaling as fast as she could.

"Well, they should," Brian yelled after her.

"You can turn right back around if you're here to say what I think you're going to say," Elizabeth said as Jessica walked into her room on Saturday night.

"I just want you to listen to reason," Jessica pleaded.

Elizabeth sat down on her bed and sighed. "I'm really getting tired of this, Jessica," she said.

"Just think of it as a regular party," Jessica said calmly as she sat down next to Elizabeth.

"But it isn't just a regular party," Elizabeth said.

"You're right," Jessica said. "It's going to be a hundred million times better than a normal party. There's going to be an amazing band from Los Angeles, and the food is going to be catered by La Maison Jacques."

"That's not what I mean," Elizabeth said, leaning down to tie her sneakers. "Most parties aren't so exclusive."

"That's not true," Jessica protested. "Most parties don't include everyone in the school. You usually have to be invited."

"OK, fine," Elizabeth conceded. "But for other parties, people aren't invited and then uninvited because some guy randomly decides you're not cool. And for other parties, invitations are invitations and not orders. Do you know that Brian Boyd practically threatened me if I didn't show up tonight?"

Jessica folded her arms. "Oh, come on, Lizzie, I'm sure you were just hearing things. It's like you're so determined not to like him that everything he says is evil, according to you. He probably just really, really wants you to attend the party."

Elizabeth flopped back on the bed in frustration. "I think it's *you* who's hearing things, Jessica—or maybe I should say *refusing* to hear things. I mean, even *you're* so intimidated by him that you think something bad will happen to you if I don't show up."

"I'm not *intimidated* by him," Jessica insisted. "I just want him to *like* me. There's a big difference."

Elizabeth sat up and groaned. "Listen, I don't have the energy to argue with you anymore. I'm not going, and that's that."

"So what are you going to do? Stay home and read depressing books like that one about that girl during the war?"

"As a matter of fact, I'm going to another party," Elizabeth said.

"Really? Whose party?"

"Mine," Elizabeth said, standing up. "And I have to go get ready."

"What kind of party are you having?"

"A party for everyone who Brian rejected," Elizabeth said. "And it's going to be a lot more fun than the one you're going to."

Eleven

"I planned something special for tomorrow," Mr. Kramer said on Saturday night. He was in the kitchen, making potato pancakes for dinner. Aaron was sitting at the kitchen table, spending a little time with his grandfather before he left for Brian's.

"You did?" Aaron asked uncertainly. Brian had asked him and some other members of *IN* to go to the mall the next day.

"I thought you and I could go fishing together like we used to do when you came to visit in New Jersey," Mr. Kramer said, smiling broadly. "I rented a little boat at a lake about an hour from here."

"That sounds really great," Aaron said quietly, "but I—"

"I knew you'd be pleased," Mr. Kramer said, as he dropped some grated-potato mixture into a skillet. "We should go to sleep early so we'll be well rested."

Aaron swallowed the lump in his throat. He felt incredibly guilty. His grandfather was so excited about the fishing trip, and in a way, Aaron really wanted to hang out with him, the way they used to. But he couldn't explain that to Brian—Brian definitely didn't like it when people turned down invitations or backed out of plans.

Aaron took a deep breath. "Um . . . well . . . listen, Grandpa, the fishing trip sounds like a blast and everything, but . . . unfortunately, I won't be able to go," he stammered.

Grandpa looked up from the table. "But I already rented the boat, and I even made some fried chicken to take for lunch."

Aaron bit his lip, trying to ignore his guilt. "I have to work on a project for social studies class," he lied. "I'm really sorry, but I have to do this thing."

"Well, if you must, you must," Mr. Kramer said. "What's the project about?"

"It's about the Holocaust," Aaron said. In fact, he *did* have to do a project on the Holocaust, but he didn't have a clue what he was going to do. He'd barely done any of his reading assignments yet—he'd been too busy with Brian and the club.

Mr. Kramer nodded gravely. "That's very important," he said. "That's worth missing the trip for. We'll do it another time."

"I knew you'd understand," Aaron said, feeling relieved and ashamed at the same time.

"Tonight at dinner, I'll tell you something about the Holocaust that you don't know," Mr. Kramer went on.

Aaron looked at the clock on the wall. Brian had told him to be at his house by six o'clock, and that was five minutes away. "Um, actually, I'm not going to be able to have dinner here tonight either," Aaron said.

Mr. Kramer raised his eyebrows. "But I've made all this food."

"It really looks great, but I have to go to a friend's house and start working on the project," Aaron said quietly.

"Then take some food with you for you and your friend," Mr. Kramer said. He got out a brown paper bag and filled it with fried chicken and rolls.

As he watched his grandfather pack up the food, Aaron felt a wave of sadness. He could just imagine walking into Brian's house with that fried chicken. Brian would laugh him right out of the party.

"Here, you go," Mr. Kramer said, handing Aaron the bag. "Enjoy it, and don't worry about tonight."

"Thanks," Aaron said quickly, standing up. "Good night."

"Aaron, help the guys from the restaurant pass the food around," Brian commanded.

"Uh . . . well, OK," Aaron said. He was standing with Jessica by the pool and feeling incredibly embarrassed. Ever since Aaron had arrived that evening, Brian had been telling him what to do. *But I guess it's an honor to be his Special Assistant,* he told himself. *Brian wouldn't want me to help out if he didn't like me.*

Aaron looked around at Brian's amazing backyard. Tables were set up all over the huge lawn, and there were a lot of lanterns and fountains. The band was great, and waiters walked around carrying food on silver platters. *It's really amazing to be here,* Aaron thought. *I'm lucky to be a part of it.*

"Brian sure seems to depend on you," Jessica said, looking at Aaron admiringly as he took a tray of tiny crab cakes. "I guess you've become really good friends."

"Oh, yeah, absolutely," Aaron replied coolly as he began to walk around with the silver platter.

"It's so sweet of him to throw a party like this for everyone," Jessica continued, following Aaron around the lawn. "He's such a great guy."

"Mmm-hmm," Aaron mumbled, trying to keep the tray balanced as a group of kids swarmed around him, reaching for the crab cakes.

"I wish Elizabeth could see all this," Jessica went on. "She really thinks Brian's a bad guy. She even said he tried to threaten her if she didn't show up. Can you imagine? I mean, obviously Brian's way too generous and charming to threaten my sister."

At the mention of Elizabeth, Aaron suddenly felt really weak. He'd been trying to put what happened that morning out of his mind, but he had to admit that it *did* seem as if Brian was threatening her. Aaron set the tray down on a table. "Listen, Jessica," he began, "maybe you should tell Elizabeth to apologize to Brian."

Jessica looked alarmed. "For what? What did she do?"

"Well . . . she . . . she said she wasn't impressed by his club," Aaron stammered. "And she called it stupid."

Jessica's eyes widened. "She didn't tell me about that," she said, looking shocked. "I can't believe she would insult him like that."

"I guess she's entitled to her own opinion," Aaron said awkwardly. "But Brian's not the kind of guy you'd want for an enemy."

"Come on, man." Brian walked up and punched Aaron playfully on the shoulder. "Pick up that tray and keep serving."

"Oh, right, sorry," Aaron said quickly.

"Hey, Jessica, this is a great song," Brian said. "Let's dance."

Aaron picked up the platter of crab cakes and watched as Brian and Jessica walked over to the dance floor together—hand in hand.

"This pizza is so yummy," Amy said, taking a gooey bite in the Wakefields' family room.

It was Saturday night, and Elizabeth and her friends were sitting on the floor surrounded by paper plates and pizza boxes.

"Well, it's not La Maison Jacques, but it's pretty good," Elizabeth responded, helping herself to a second slice with peppers and onions.

"I wonder what's going on at Brian's party right now," Maria mused.

Anna shrugged. "I guess they're all dancing to that famous band."

"Well, I'm glad I'm here instead of there," Amy said smiling at Elizabeth. "I mean, you've been to one party at a mansion that has a pool and a famous band and food from La Maison Jacques and you've been to them all, right?"

Melissa giggled. "I'm really glad to be here, too, but I can't help wondering why I'm not good enough for Brian's party."

"I know what you mean," Winston said.

Elizabeth looked around at her friends with distress. She had had enough of everyone feeling bad about themselves because of Brian Boyd. "Do you all think there's anything wrong with the way you are or the way anyone else in this room is?" she asked the group.

Everyone looked around the room at one another.

"No, not really," Winston said sheepishly.

"If you were going to have a party, wouldn't you invite every person here?" Elizabeth pressed.

"Yeah, of course I would," Anna responded, as the other guests nodded.

"So just think about this guy Brian," Elizabeth said. "Look how he's made all of you doubt yourselves."

"That's true," Maria said. "Usually, I'm a pretty confident person. Since Brian started his club, I've been wondering what I could've done that made him not like me."

"And think about Brian," Elizabeth went on. "Everyone talks about how cool and popular he is. But do any of you really think he's such a great guy? Has he been nice to any of you?"

For another long moment, everyone looked at everyone else in silence.

Finally, Anna took a deep breath. "Actually, he did something yesterday that was really mean."

"What did he do?" Amy asked, leaning forward.

"When I walked into math class, he started pretending to do sign language," Anna said. "He waved his hands around in the air and made people laugh."

Elizabeth's cheeks grew warm, and her heart was racing. "That's absolutely horrible!"

"Did you tell the teacher?" Amy asked.

"No, I was too embarrassed to make a big deal out of it," Anna said. "I thought maybe he was just being funny—like maybe I was being too sensitive. I mean, he obviously likes to joke around."

Elizabeth shook her head. "You're not being too

sensitive. He likes to be funny, all right—funny at other people's expense."

"He really *is* a creep," Melissa said in disgust. "I can't believe I actually wanted to help that guy get ready for his stupid party."

"Brian even did something to me the other day that I didn't tell anyone about," Amy confessed softly.

"Tell us," Elizabeth said.

"When I was standing in the lunch line, he stood behind me and started barking," Amy said quietly.

"What's that supposed to mean?" Melissa asked.

Amy took a deep breath. "I guess it means I'm ugly as a dog. I didn't really get it at the time because—well, I guess because I didn't want to. It just seemed too unbelievably horrible, and everyone seemed to think he was so great, so I figured I must be misinterpreting. But now that I think about it, and now that I hear about the stuff he's done to everyone else—well, I can totally see him making fun of me like that."

"Amy, you're beautiful," Elizabeth said, standing up. She didn't know if she could hear much more. Every story put her closer and closer to the edge. "You're all wonderful, great people. This Brian Boyd has to be stopped once and for all!"

Winston's eyes widened. "What do you mean? How are you going to stop him? He's going to be more popular than ever after that party tonight."

"We're going to start spreading the word that

he's a rotten person," Elizabeth declared. "We'll make people see that they're better off not being in his club, and soon there won't be a club anymore."

An uncomfortable silence fell over the room. Elizabeth could almost hear her own heart beating. "Maria? Winston? Amy? Anyone?"

"I think that's a really great idea, Elizabeth," Amy said softly, "but, well, I keep thinking about what my cousin Emily said—you know, about how Brian's not a good person to have on your bad side."

"But what can he do?" Elizabeth asked. "He's only a sixth-grade jerk."

Winston looked at the ground. "I don't know, Elizabeth. He just seems so—powerful. I don't think I can risk having him as an enemy."

Elizabeth looked around at her friends—they all looked meek and helpless, and she realized how terrified of Brian they were. "OK, then, I'll do it myself," she said firmly. "Pretty soon *IN* won't exist, and Brian Boyd will wish he'd never set foot in our school!"

Twelve

Elizabeth walked down the hall on Monday morning feeling as though she were in a bad movie. Everyone stopped and looked at her as she passed by them as if she had some dread disease or something. When she walked to the water fountain to get a drink, the crowd of people standing around it quickly dispersed.

After taking a drink of water, Elizabeth spotted Jessica standing by some lockers with Lila and Janet.

"Hey, you guys," Elizabeth said cautiously as she walked up to them.

"Later, Jessica," Janet said, walking off.

"See ya," Lila added, following Janet.

Elizabeth stared at her sister. "What's going on? Is it my blouse?" For the first time since *IN* was formed, Elizabeth wasn't wearing a black T-shirt.

"What you're doing is a whole lot worse than violating the dress code," Jessica said through clenched teeth.

"What are you talking about?"

"Word is going around that you're on a campaign to bad mouth Brian and the club," Jessica whispered.

Elizabeth took a deep breath. "Boy, word really travels fast around here."

"Why didn't you tell me you were planning this?" Jessica hissed.

Elizabeth rolled her eyes. "Why? So you could try to talk me out of it? I figured I'd save you the trouble. I think people should know the truth about Brian Boyd."

"Shhhhh," Jessica warned. She looked around the hall nervously. "Brian told all of us not to talk to you. He called an emergency meeting this morning before school."

Elizabeth folded her arms. "From the way you're acting, it seems like you're afraid to be seen talking to me, too."

Jessica stared at Elizabeth. "You're making things really hard for me, you know? Nobody wants to have anything to do with you. You're my twin sister, and I'm obviously not going to ignore you, but you have to understand if I don't want to be seen—"

"Spending time with me?" Elizabeth finished

Jessica's sentence. "Jessica, how can you let yourself be controlled by that guy?"

"Keep your voice down," Jessica commanded, looking nervously around, as people began to stop and stare.

"No, I won't keep my voice down," Elizabeth said, raising her voice. "You and everyone else in this school are being brainwashed by Brian Boyd, and I'm not going to stand around and pretend I don't see it."

Elizabeth heard someone clapping loudly and slowly behind her. She turned around and saw Brian smiling widely.

"Bravo!" Brian said. "That's really impressive! I've never heard such a paranoid person before!"

"I'm glad you enjoyed it," Elizabeth said bitterly. She was aware that the crowd around them was growing bigger, though no one said a word. "I hope everyone else is just as impressed when they find out what you're really like."

"And what's that?" Brian asked smugly. "What am I really like?"

Elizabeth's heart was pounding wildly and she spat out the words. "You're bigoted and elitist—"

"And a brainwasher, too, right? I kind of like that idea," Brian broke in. "It sounds like we're in a science-fiction movie."

The crowd rippled with laughter. Elizabeth was trying to hold back the tears.

"This was supposed to be a project for class, and

you've turned it into something evil," Elizabeth said, feeling her whole body shaking.

"So now I'm evil, boys and girls," Brian said, laughing. "Maybe you should just call me the big bad wolf."

Elizabeth was too angry and upset to speak. She pushed her way through the crowd of laughing people, feeling as if she were in a living nightmare.

Aaron turned the page of his book, feeling chills up and down his spine. He was sitting in the library during his free period on Monday afternoon, reading about the Holocaust for his history project.

He felt sick to his stomach. He'd been reading how the Nazis collaborated with Hitler to do unspeakable things to Jews. Jews were sent to concentration camps and separated from their families. Jewish prisoners had numbers tattooed on their arms. They died horrible, excruciating deaths. Aaron had always told himself that the Holocaust was something in the past, but somehow, as he read about it now, the tragedy felt real and present.

"Aaron, come here a minute," Brian whispered urgently from a nearby stack of books.

Aaron jumped a little at the sound of Brian's voice. All the while he'd been reading, school and Brian and *IN* had seemed far off.

Automatically, he got up and walked over to where Brian was standing. "What's up?" he whispered.

Brian looked around to make sure nobody was close by. "You have to help me get Elizabeth Wakefield."

Aaron felt his heart race as he remembered the scene between Brian and Elizabeth in the hallway that morning. He had laughed along with everyone, even though the whole thing seemed awful and scary.

"I think you already did a good job of telling her what you think today," Aaron said quietly, hoping that would satisfy Brian. "I doubt you'll have any more problems from her."

"She's spreading terrible stories around the school about me," Brian said. "She has to be stopped."

Aaron shuddered as he looked at Brian's face. It was handsome on the outside, but there was something evil in his eyes. *Evil,* Aaron thought. *Just like Elizabeth said.* Aaron looked away, hoping Brian would just leave him alone.

Brian stepped a little closer and gripped Aaron's shoulder with his hand. Aaron felt his breathing grow short.

"Since you're my Special Assistant," Brian said slowly and deliberately, "I'll need your help."

Aaron's lip began to quiver. He felt he had no choice but to listen to Brian. "What do you want me to do?" he asked helplessly.

"Tell Elizabeth to meet you at her locker at three-thirty this afternoon. You want some help working on your class project," Brian said.

"And then what?"

"You're going to meet me at the water fountain at three twenty-five," Brian said. "Oh, and bring someone from the club along with you in case we need help. Try Kimberly Haver. Yeah, she's a helpful kind of girl, right?"

"What are we going to do?" Aaron asked, hearing the quaver in his own voice.

"You'll see," Brian said. "Just make sure Elizabeth's there."

Elizabeth walked down the hall to her locker, where she was supposed to meet Aaron to go over his social studies project. She couldn't help feeling weird. After all, Aaron was practically Brian's best friend. But he'd been so nice when he asked her—apologetic, even. *Maybe he wants to confide in me about Brian,* she thought. *He's probably on my side and wants to help me put an end to all the awfulness that Brian started.*

Elizabeth opened her locker to get some books she'd need that night. She looked at her watch. It was exactly three thirty. No one was around, since school had ended a half hour before.

"This will teach you a lesson!"

Elizabeth turned around and saw Aaron, Brian, and Kimberly Haver coming toward her. Before she could do anything, Brian grabbed her arms.

"Let go of me!" she shrieked. Brian twisted her

right arm behind her back and tried shoving her in the locker face forward. "You're hurting my arm! Aaron, tell him to stop!"

Brian glanced behind him as footsteps sounded down the hall.

"Hey, what's going on?"

"Jessica!" Elizabeth shouted tearfully as she heard her sister's voice.

"Let's get out of here," Brian hissed, throwing Elizabeth to the floor. He, Aaron, and Kimberly quickly ran down the hall.

Elizabeth sat trembling on the floor, tears running down her face. She clutched her bruised arm.

"Elizabeth! What happened?" Jessica asked frantically.

Elizabeth was crying so hard she could barely get the words out. "Your hero, Brian Boyd, just attacked me!" she yelled.

"Oh, Lizzie, I'm so sorry," Jessica said as she knelt down beside her.

"What do you think of him now?" Elizabeth asked angrily.

Aaron ran up the front steps to his house with tears running down his face. He was filled with self-disgust. *How could I have left Elizabeth crying on the ground like that?* he wondered. *It's like Brian has turned me into some horrible monster!*

All he wanted was to talk to his grandfather. Mr. Kramer was wise and loving, and he would listen to the whole story. His grandfather would know what to do.

"Grandpa!" he called out desperately. He ran into the kitchen, but Mr. Kramer wasn't there. "Grandpa!" he yelled again, running into the family room to see if his grandfather was watching television. The family room was empty.

Aaron ran up the stairs two at a time and flung open the door to the guest room. "Grandpa!" Aaron cried, the tears nearly choking him when he saw his grandfather lying in bed, taking a nap. "Grandpa, wake up!"

Thirteen

Mr. Kramer opened his eyes and looked at Aaron with concern. "What's wrong, my boy?" he asked as he sat up.

"Grandpa," Aaron said between sobs, "I'm so sorry." He threw his arms around his grandfather and held on tight.

"You're sorry about what, my boy?" Mr. Kramer said kindly. "Tell me what has happened."

"Grandpa, something horrible . . ." Aaron started between sobs. "I did something . . . terrible. . . ."

"What do you mean?" Mr. Kramer asked. "Slow down. I'm sure it's not all that bad."

"This horrible boy, Brian, started this club," Aaron started to explain.

"The club you told me about that you were so excited to be in?" Mr. Kramer asked.

"That's right," Aaron said. "I thought it was so great and cool, and I was suddenly so popular."

"But what went wrong?" Mr. Kramer asked.

Aaron tried to get control of his breathing. "He started doing all this bad stuff. Like making people feel rotten just for the fun of it, and kicking people out just because—just because they were different from him."

"Different? In what way different?" Mr. Kramer pressed.

"Well, he wouldn't let this sweet girl Anna be in the club because she's hearing-impaired," Aaron began. He was putting things together for the first time—he was seeing everything he'd been afraid to see. "And he kicked another girl out because her family doesn't have a lot of money. And he was mean to a lot of really nice people who maybe weren't considered beautiful or cool. And he—he got people to just go along with him." Aaron put his face in his hands. "I can't believe it—I can't believe I did all that."

Mr. Kramer stroked Aaron's head. "What did you do, my boy?" he asked gently.

"I helped him," Aaron blurted out. "I told the people they couldn't be in the club. I even—"

"What? What did you do?"

"I even helped him try to throw this girl in her locker right now just because she was saying things about Brian," Aaron said. "Things that were true."

"You collaborated with him," Mr. Kramer said slowly.

Aaron looked up at Mr. Kramer. *Collaborated*. He repeated the word to himself. That was the word he had read in that book about the Holocaust—people had collaborated with the Nazis, who did all those horrible things to the Jews.

Suddenly, everything became terrifyingly clear. *That's what the game was all about*, he realized. Brian was this horrible, powerful leader, and so many people at Sweet Valley Middle School had collaborated with him! "Grandpa, when you said something like the Holocaust could happen at any place, anytime—you were right!"

Mr. Kramer nodded, stroking Aaron's head. "Aaron, my boy, I want to show you something."

Slowly, Grandpa pulled up his sleeve and held out his left arm for Aaron to see.

Aaron looked down. Numbers were tattooed on the back of his grandfather's arm, just above the wrist.

Aaron's sense of horror was so great, he couldn't breathe. "Your arm," he said finally. "The numbers. The Holocaust." How come he had never noticed the numbers before? His grandpa must have been careful to keep them hidden.

Grandpa's eyes filled with tears. "Yes, the Nazis put these numbers here. They are a reminder of the horror that I saw."

"But I never knew," Aaron said, shaking. "You never told me."

"That's what I was going to tell you on Saturday night," Mr. Kramer said. "I thought you were old enough now to know."

"Is that how you lost your family?" Aaron asked, as the tears started flowing down his face.

Grandpa swallowed hard and nodded. "Everyone in my family was killed in the concentration camp. Everyone except me."

Aaron thought about his own family. He didn't see how he could go on living if his mother and father were killed.

"How old were you when you were there?" Aaron asked.

"Twelve years old," Mr. Kramer said. "Exactly your age."

Aaron threw his arms around him. "I'm so sorry that happened to you," he said, sobbing. "I'm so sorry you lost your family and I'm so sorry I've let you down. . . . I'm just as bad as those evil Nazis. . . ."

Grandpa put his finger over Aaron's mouth. "Hush," he said gently. "You're not like those Nazis. But you have learned a very important lesson—a lesson you'll never forget."

"I feel like I want to move away from here," Aaron said tearfully. "Everything is too horrible."

"It's not too late to make things better," Mr. Kramer said, consoling him.

"Grandpa, I love you," Aaron said as he collapsed in tears.

"I love you, too." Grandpa cradled Aaron in his arms and rocked him back and forth.

"Can I have your attention," Mr. Levin said in front of social studies class on Tuesday morning. "Today, Aaron Dallas wants to make a special presentation for his project."

Aaron walked to the front of the class. He took a deep breath and looked around the room. All the members of *IN* were still wearing black T-shirts and black armbands—all but Elizabeth and Aaron.

"I want to tell you about my hero," Aaron said proudly. "Grandpa, could you come here?"

Mr. Kramer walked to the front of the room and sat down in a chair, facing the class.

"This is my Grandpa," Aaron announced. "His name is Saul Kramer, and he's a Holocaust survivor."

Gasps echoed around the room.

"Grandpa, could you tell us what happened to you and your family?"

"When I was twelve years old, my family was living in Vienna, Austria," Mr. Kramer began. "My father was a conductor for the symphony, and my mother was a violinist. One day, we learned that Hitler's Nazis had taken over our city. Nobody really knew what that meant. At first, the only thing that changed was that we had to wear big gold stars wherever we went."

"Why did you have to wear stars?" Maria asked.

"To show that we were Jewish," Grandpa explained. "At my school, there were only a few other boys who were also Jewish. After the Nazis came, nobody would sit at the lunch table with us, so we all started sitting together. We were asked to use a separate boys' room, and in our classroom, our desks were put in the corner together."

Aaron looked around the room. Every student was hanging on his grandfather's words. The only person who looked unmoved was Brian.

"One day I came home from school, and all the things in our house were packed in boxes and suitcases," Grandpa said. "I asked my mother what was happening, and she said that the Nazis were sending us away somewhere. I asked her where, but she said she didn't know.

"We went to the train station and got on a train that was so filled with people you could barely move. It was dark, and you couldn't see the person next to you. We were packed in like animals.

"It seemed that we were on the train for days. Nobody knew where we were going. Finally, we arrived at our destination—Bergen-Belsen."

"Isn't that the concentration camp where Anne Frank was?" Elizabeth asked.

"That's right," Grandpa said. "She died there just two months before the end of the war."

"And what happened to your family?" Elizabeth asked.

"When we got off the train, my sisters—Rachel, Sarah, and Anna—were taken to the section for women with my mother," Mr. Kramer responded, his voice cracking. "That was the last time I ever saw them."

"Mr. Kramer, you can stop now if you want to," Mr. Levin said gently. "I know this must be very upsetting for you."

"No, it's important to tell my story," Grandpa said. "It's important for people to know, so it won't happen again."

"Then, please, continue," Mr. Levin said.

"My father and I were sent to the part of the camp for men," Mr. Kramer went on. "Two days after we got there, my father was sent to the gas chamber, where he died. Two weeks later, my mother and sisters were also sent there to die. I am here only because Bergen-Belsen was liberated before they killed me."

The classroom was still and silent. Most of the students had tears in their eyes.

Aaron walked back to the front of the room. "I want to talk about right now. I realized yesterday why Mr. Levin's game was about the Holocaust." He took a deep breath. "Yesterday, Brian and I tried to throw Elizabeth Wakefield into her locker," he confessed.

The classroom filled with whispers and gasps.

"We were going to lock her inside," Aaron continued. "And the reason we were going to do that was— Actually, Brian why don't you stand up."

Brian looked casually around the room. He didn't move from his seat.

"Brian, stand up," Mr. Levin instructed.

Brian stood up slowly and folded his arms in front of him. "Yeah, so?"

"Why don't you tell everyone why you wanted to throw Elizabeth in her locker," Mr. Levin said.

"I didn't," Brian said defensively. "That's a lie."

"Elizabeth, did he try to throw you in your locker?" Mr. Levin asked.

"Yes, he did," Elizabeth said quietly.

"I'll tell you why," Aaron said. "Elizabeth was the only person who dared to tell the truth about Brian and his club."

"And what was the truth?" Mr. Levin asked.

"That people who were—who were *different* from what Brian was couldn't be in the club," Aaron said loudly and clearly. "That Brian was elitist and prejudiced. That he threatened people who didn't follow his orders exactly. That people listened to him and looked up to him because he seemed cool and powerful, without really looking at the kind of person he was."

Aaron looked around the classroom. One by one, students took off their armbands and gave Brian dirty looks.

"I was just as guilty as Brian for going along with him," Aaron went on. "I refused to see what was really going on, because I was so impressed by the power he had. Eventually, when I did start having doubts about him, I was afraid that he might do something to me if I didn't go along with him."

"I think what Aaron just said is the most important lesson of all," Mr. Levin said. "The Nazis did what Hitler told them to do without questioning whether or not it was evil."

"But why would they do whatever Hitler told them to do?" Maria asked.

"Because they were impressed by his power and how important he made them feel," Mr. Levin explained. "And because of fear. They were afraid of what could happen to them if they didn't follow his wishes."

"That's exactly what happened to me during the game," Aaron announced.

"I don't think you're the only one that happened to," Mr. Levin said, looking around the room.

"It happened to me, too," Jessica spoke up loudly.

"Can you tell us about it?" Mr. Levin prompted.

Jessica stood up and looked right at Elizabeth. "I was trying to force my sister to go along with Brian and his club even though she didn't want to. I was even afraid to be seen talking to her in public after it got out that she was saying bad things about Brian. I was so—so, I guess, into Brian's power, and excited to be a part of his club, that I didn't even pay any attention when Elizabeth started getting really upset." She bit her lip as if she were trying to fight back tears. "I'm sorry, Lizzie."

Elizabeth stood up and put her arms around Jessica. "It's OK," she said. "It's all over now."

"No, it's not OK," Jessica said, turning to the class. "When I found her lying on the ground after Brian attacked her, I felt like it was all my fault."

"But it wasn't all your fault," Mr. Levin said. "It was everybody's fault."

"It was Brian's fault," Amy yelled out.

"Hey, I'm not taking all the blame for this," Brian protested hotly. "I was only doing what Mr. Levin told me to do."

"Brian's right, to a point," Mr. Levin said. "He was doing what I told him to do. He just took things a lot further than I'd intended. Obviously, things got really out of control, and I didn't realize it."

"See?" Brian said defensively. "Even the teacher says I'm not responsible."

"Well, Brian, I think you need to do a lot of thinking about what drove you to such extremes," Mr. Levin said sternly. "Your behavior throughout this whole game was frightening, and I'm going to have to call your parents in for a conference about your prejudiced and threatening behavior."

"That's not fair," Brian said. "I was just doing my assignment for school."

"We'll talk about this later with your parents," Mr. Levin said briskly.

Brian's face turned bright red as he slumped down in his seat, crossing his arms in front of him.

Mr. Levin turned to Aaron and Mr. Kramer. "Thank you for sharing this with us today." He looked back at the class. "This game is obviously over. I think you've all learned the lesson I was hoping you would—and then some!"

"Oh, there's one more thing," Aaron said. "I want to apologize to everyone that I hurt and excluded." He looked straight at Elizabeth. "And I especially want to apologize to you, Elizabeth. And to thank you. I think it's great the way you stood up for yourself and what you believe in."

Then he turned toward his grandfather, who clutched him in a hug. "I'm very proud of you," Mr. Kramer said.

"Not as proud as I am of you," Aaron responded.

"I'd never thought I'd say this," Jessica said to Mandy as they walked out of school at the end of the day. "But I'm ready to go back to the regular kind of schoolwork—books and papers and stuff. No more games for me."

Mandy nodded. "Tell me about it. And I don't think I ever want to hear the word *party* again."

"Hey, don't go *that* far," Jessica protested. "I happen to know of a really great party that you *have* to go to."

"Really? Whose?"

"Mine!" Jessica exclaimed. "Elizabeth and Mom and I are having this great mother-daughter brunch to celebrate Mother's Day."

What will happen at the Wakefields mother-daughter brunch? Find out in Sweet Valley Twins #87, **The Mother-Daughter Switch**.

Bantam Books in the SWEET VALLEY TWINS series.
Ask your bookseller for the books you have missed.

#1 BEST FRIENDS
#2 TEACHER'S PET
#3 THE HAUNTED HOUSE
#4 CHOOSING SIDES
#5 SNEAKING OUT
#6 THE NEW GIRL
#7 THREE'S A CROWD
#8 FIRST PLACE
#9 AGAINST THE RULES
#10 ONE OF THE GANG
#11 BURIED TREASURE
#12 KEEPING SECRETS
#13 STRETCHING THE TRUTH
#14 TUG OF WAR
#15 THE OLDER BOY
#16 SECOND BEST
#17 BOYS AGAINST GIRLS
#18 CENTER OF ATTENTION
#19 THE BULLY
#20 PLAYING HOOKY
#21 LEFT BEHIND
#22 OUT OF PLACE
#23 CLAIM TO FAME
#24 JUMPING TO CONCLUSIONS
#25 STANDING OUT
#26 TAKING CHARGE
#27 TEAMWORK
#28 APRIL FOOL!
#29 JESSICA AND THE BRAT ATTACK
#30 PRINCESS ELIZABETH
#31 JESSICA'S BAD IDEA
#32 JESSICA ON STAGE
#33 ELIZABETH'S NEW HERO
#34 JESSICA, THE ROCK STAR
#35 AMY'S PEN PAL
#36 MARY IS MISSING
#37 THE WAR BETWEEN THE TWINS
#38 LOIS STRIKES BACK
#39 JESSICA AND THE MONEY MIX-UP
#40 DANNY MEANS TROUBLE
#41 THE TWINS GET CAUGHT
#42 JESSICA'S SECRET
#43 ELIZABETH'S FIRST KISS
#44 AMY MOVES IN

Sweet Valley Twins Super Editions

#1 THE CLASS TRIP
#2 HOLIDAY MISCHIEF
#3 THE BIG CAMP SECRET
#4 THE UNICORNS GO HAWAIIAN
#5 LILA'S SECRET VALENTINE

Sweet Valley Twins Super Chiller Editions

#1 THE CHRISTMAS GHOST
#2 THE GHOST IN THE GRAVEYARD
#3 THE CARNIVAL GHOST
#4 THE GHOST IN THE BELL TOWER
#5 THE CURSE OF THE RUBY NECKLACE
#6 THE CURSE OF THE GOLDEN HEART
#7 THE HAUNTED BURIAL GROUND

Sweet Valley Twins Magna Editions

THE MAGIC CHRISTMAS
BIG FOR CHRISTMAS
A CHRISTMAS WITHOUT ELIZABETH

#45 LUCY TAKES THE REINS
#46 MADEMOISELLE JESSICA
#47 JESSICA'S NEW LOOK
#48 MANDY MILLER FIGHTS BACK
#49 THE TWINS' LITTLE SISTER
#50 JESSICA AND THE SECRET STAR
#51 ELIZABETH THE IMPOSSIBLE
#52 BOOSTER BOYCOTT
#53 THE SLIME THAT ATE SWEET VALLEY
#54 THE BIG PARTY WEEKEND
#55 BROOKE AND HER ROCK-STAR MOM
#56 THE WAKEFIELDS STRIKE IT RICH
#57 BIG BROTHER'S IN LOVE!
#58 ELIZABETH AND THE ORPHANS
#59 BARNYARD BATTLE
#60 CIAO, SWEET VALLEY!
#61 JESSICA THE NERD
#62 SARAH'S DAD AND SOPHIA'S MOM
#63 POOR LILA!
#64 THE CHARM SCHOOL MYSTERY
#65 PATTY'S LAST DANCE
#66 THE GREAT BOYFRIEND SWITCH
#67 JESSICA THE THIEF
#68 THE MIDDLE SCHOOL GETS MARRIED
#69 WON'T SOMEONE HELP ANNA?
#70 PSYCHIC SISTERS
#71 JESSICA SAVES THE TREES
#72 THE LOVE POTION
#73 LILA'S MUSIC VIDEO
#74 ELIZABETH THE HERO
#75 JESSICA AND THE EARTHQUAKE
#76 YOURS FOR A DAY
#77 TODD RUNS AWAY
#78 STEVEN THE ZOMBIE
#79 JESSICA'S BLIND DATE
#80 THE GOSSIP WAR
#81 ROBBERY AT THE MALL
#82 STEVEN'S ENEMY
#83 AMY'S SECRET SISTER
#84 ROMEO AND 2 JULIETS
#85 ELIZABETH THE SEVENTH-GRADER
#86 IT CAN'T HAPPEN HERE